Domi
The power [of?]
The perfect person is
a powerful thing
Kristi Tailor

A Winter's Kiss

By Kristi Tailor

7th Meadow Publishing

All Rights Reserved

Cover design by Les
Cover photos from Shutterstock
Book printed by CreateSpace Publishing USA

No part of this publication may be reproduced, distributed, or transmitted in any form or by any means, including photocopying, recording, or other electronic or mechanical methods, without prior written permission of the publisher, except in the case of brief quotations embodied in critical reviews and certain other noncommercial uses permitted by copyright law.

This book is a work of fiction. Names, products, characters, businesses, organizations, places, events and incidents either are the product of the author's imagination or are used fictitiously. Any resemblance to actual persons, living or dead, events, or locales is entirely coincidental.

Copyright © 2015 Kristi Tailor

All rights reserved.

ISBN:1522863230
ISBN:9781522863236

ACKNOWLEDGEMENTS AND THANKS

A special thank you to my wonderful daughter, Madison for helping me come up with a title in the late hours of night. Mommy loves you.

To my good friend, Alisha, thank you for inquiring about this novella. Knowing that even one person wanted it written meant the world to me.

To my writing partner, and dear friend Kirby Elaine, thank you for everything that you've done, will do, and are doing right now.

Thank you to my family and friends for their continual support through my writing journey.

And to my readers, thank you so much for all of your support.

Lord, thank you for blessing me continuously.

"Words hold more power than the mightiest of weapons. Use them wisely."

- Kristi Tailor

Look for *A Winter's Promise* the next novella in the A Winter's Tale series coming January 2016.

A Winter's Kiss is also available as an eBook

DEDICATION

To My Sister, Sharonne, who has always been the wind beneath my wings.

Prologue

NOVEMBER 2006

Charlotte Toutant took the stairs leading to her apartment two at a time. Tightly gripping the many grocery bags wrapped around her wrist, she mentally counted the stairs stopping when she reached the third landing. "He could have at least opened the door for me," Charlotte frowned, dropping the bags to the floor. Rummaging through her messy purse she searched in vain for her keys, they weren't there. *Where did I see them last? Dining room table, maybe?* Sighing, Charlotte knocked on the door. Once. Twice. Three times. Nothing. "Todd, really!" she groaned, beginning a new search in the endless bag for her cell phone which too was among the list of missing items. Shaking her head, she admonished herself for her careless nature. Agitated, Charlotte shook the door knob in defeat, shocked when the door opened for her. *I could have sworn that I locked the door behind me,* she shrugged, grateful that she hadn't.

Placing the grocery bags on the long counter in her kitchen Charlotte smiled to herself at the sight of her cell phone and keys on the breakfast bar to her right. Grabbing both, she walked out of the kitchen stripping her running leggings and t- shirt as she did so. The smell of sweat and outside spilled from her pores, and though she loved the natural pheromones that filled her senses after enjoying a long morning run her boyfriend did not.

Standing outside of their bedroom door Charlotte removed her sports bra and boy shorts. "Todd, didn't you hear me knocking? You could have at least helped me with–" Charlotte froze, her eyes wide, her mouth gaped open, but she couldn't speak.

"Charlotte!" Marguerite Toutant shouted, covering her naked body with the thin bed sheet.

"Damn- it!" Todd cursed jumping off the bed. "Charli, let me explain. Damn-it," he repeated.

Charlotte remained silent as if in a daze blinking rapidly as tears ran steadily down her cheeks. Not bothering to wipe them she looked past the man who slowly advanced toward her. "Marleet," she said, softly addressing her younger sister by the nickname she had given her when they were just small girls. "Why?" Charlotte asked, her voice raspy. "Why would you do this to me?"

"I'm sorry," Marguerite sobbed. "I didn't mean—"

"How long has this been going on?" Charlotte demanded.

"Char—" Marguerite began.

"How long?"

"Two years," Todd answered, stepping in front of Charlotte, blocking her view from her sister. "Charli, let's speak in the living room."

"Two years!" she yelled. "Two years! You've been sleeping with my sister for two years!" she gasped, her heart sinking deeper into her chest. "This isn't happening, it can't really be happening," she whispered, refusing to believe that the two people she trusted above all others would hurt her in such a way.

"We need to talk," Todd said quietly. "Let's go–"

"Why do we need to speak in privacy? You've done enough in private already . . . anything you have to say to me say it in front of her. It's not as if you two have anything else to hide."

Todd grabbed Charlotte by her forearm attempting to usher her out of the bedroom.

"Don't touch me," she bit through clenched teeth. Snatching away from him , Charlotte's stomach lurched, her temples pounded in protest as the reality of her nakedness became a remembered thought. Grimacing, she backed out of the room, and took off down the hall to where her damp clothes lay in a heap on the floor.

Todd followed her into the living room pulling on his boxer briefs as he did so. "I didn't want you to find out like this," he explained, walking up behind her. "I was going to tell you after the holidays."

"How kind of you," she laughed sarcastically. "After the holidays, huh, was that supposed to make it better . . . less awkward at Thanksgiving dinner . . . pretending in front of our families on Christmas– going through the routine . . . before telling me that you've been screwing my sister? If you think I'm going to just forgive you like none of this ever happened, you're wrong. I'm not going to stay with you after this. I–"

"I wasn't going to ask you to," Todd sighed.

"What?"

"Charlotte . . . Marguerite and I are getting married."

"What?"

Todd took a step toward her. "I asked her to marry me. She wanted to tell you, but I told her not to. I wanted to be the one to give you the news."

"What?" she choked, exasperated.

"I know it seems like a lot to ask, but I really need for you to be supportive. Your sister loves you, and hurting you was the last thing she ever wanted to do."

"Is this a sick joke? Like are there cameras recording us right now?" she asked, bewildered. "Todd we've been together for seven years . . . we've been discussing marriage . . . how many kids we wanted to have . . . where we wanted to retire . . . we've built a life together, and now you're telling me that you are going to marry my little sister. What sense does that make?"

"I'm sorry. I can't help who I love."

"You can't help who you love?" she laughed bitterly. "That's your reasoning, really? You disgust me."

"I'm sorry."

"Stop saying you're sorry," she squealed angrily. You're not sorry," Charlotte hissed as the new onslaught of tears began to pour from her eyes. Shaking her head she wiped viciously at her damp cheeks. "My parents are never going to accept this," she snorted. "So if you think your life with her is going to be easy, you can forget it."

Todd hunched his shoulders letting out a small breath as he stared at her in silence.

Laughing uncontrollably, Charlotte narrowed her eyes at the man she loved. She knew his body language well. "They know?" she said more as a realization than a question.

"Yes," he answered.

"So everyone knew except for me?"

Silence.

"Answer me! Everyone has known that the two of you have been having an affair behind my back, and no one has had the decency to fill me in? My mom and dad have known the entire time, that's the reality? That's the truth?" More than anything she needed for him to denounce her accusations. She needed for him to say that her parents were innocent of knowing about her sister's betrayal. More than anything she needed for them to be blameless.

Silence.

"Tell your fiancé that she's dead to me," Charlotte cried before turning away from him. Feeling broken and alone she walked away from the only man she had ever loved.

Chapter One

NOVEMBER 2008

Charlotte kept a steady pace as she ran through the streets of Manhattan. Turning on East 1st street, she took long strides quickly reaching Bowery, reveling in the early morning dew as the autumn breeze caressed her damp skin. The feel of her heart pounding wildly in her chest brought on a wave of exhilaration that sprung through her nerve endings giving her body the sudden push needed to continue down the long blocks. Reaching 7th street Charlotte adjusted the heavy backpack that bounced on her long back, the continual friction causing a sensitized spot to form there. Still, she pushed onward passing 9th street and rounding Tompkins Square Park at Avenue B in record time.

Charlotte loved running through the crowded streets of New York City. There was so much life budding around her, different smells greeted her on every corner from family owned restaurants and street vendors. Smiling as she passed people from different walks of life standing side by side on a narrow curb, Charlotte thought about the morning runs she had taken back in Baltimore. *Maryland and New York are like night and day*, she mused.

Uprooting her life and making the move to Manhattan had surprisingly been an easy transition. After only two weeks of job searching she landed a temp position with *Leisure Me Ready* magazine working under Editor- in-Chief, Nicholas Elliot, as his over- zealous receptionist. Though she felt fortunate in finding a job as quickly as she had the repetitiveness of her duties bored her beyond reason. With a background in teaching high school English Literature Charlotte was use to the fast pace of being in a classroom, and the spontaneity of thinking on her feet, two traits that she thought made her well equipped to apply for the Editorial position that opened up a few weeks after being employed with the company. With little hope in obtaining the position, she was beyond ecstatic when Nicholas called her into his office to discuss her salary, and employee benefits. In that moment, Charlotte felt that her life was finally moving forward in a positive direction; the emotional rollercoaster she had been on was seemingly slowing down.

Pushing through the large glass doors Charlotte's long legs took lengthy strides as she crossed the large foyer. "Good morning," she said, greeting a group of women who stood idly behind the receptionist desk.

"Good morning Ms. Toutant," they said in unison snickering quietly as she walked past them. Charlotte frowned inwardly knowing the meaning behind their cattiness. As rumor had it around the office she was the *harlot* who had seduced the boss, hence, assuring her position as Editor. Charlotte shook her head as she boarded the elevator. It amazed her how vicious women could be toward one another. True, she was promoted rather quickly, but to automatically assume that her advancement was due to an affair with her boss was a disgusting accusation.

"Ms. Toutant!" Emily, a short robust woman ran after her. "Ms. Toutant! Wait a sec," she heaved, seemingly out of breath as she threw herself into the opening of the elevator, stopping the doors from closing.

"Yes?" Charlotte smiled politely. "Are you okay?" she asked the older woman.

"I'll be fine. Mr. Elliot wants you to meet him in the conference room."

"The conference room? I thought he was scheduled to hold a meeting with the Board of Directors this morning?"

"He's meeting with them now."

"And he requested for me to meet him there?" Charlotte asked, confusion evident in her tone.

"Yes ma'am."

Was I supposed to have something prepared for him? She wondered, anxiety quickly overtaking her. "Thank you, Emily," she said sweetly. "Go take a seat, and rest yourself for a moment. I don't like the way you're breathing."

"I'll be fine," the other woman assured her. "Good luck in your meeting."

"Thanks," she smiled as the elevator doors closed. "I'm going to need it."

Chapter Two

Charlotte stood outside of the conference room awaiting the right moment to enter.

"The magazine industry isn't what it used to be. Years ago people spent their last on the latest gossip magazines wanting to know what was happening with their favorite celebrities, and wanting to stay clued in on the entertainment world, but times have changed. The same information they can read in magazines, they can receive for free over the internet," Dean Proctor explained.

Rolling her eyes Charlotte sighed at her co-worker's No- It- All disposition. Not that he would have ever known, but Charlotte secretly despised working with the man. Dean Proctor had been introduced to her as the Lead of Financial Affairs, though, over the months he made the knowledge clear that he involved himself in other factors of the company both business oriented, and personal; while she had no definite proof that he was the one behind the rumors that had quickly spread around the office, she was confident in her supposition. Plucking her short black hair from behind her ears Charlotte took several deep breaths. *Geez Nick, why couldn't you give me a heads up?* She thought. Pushing open the large glass doors Charlotte sashayed past the silent onlookers with her head held high, and a small smirk on her ruby painted lips; though outwardly poised Charlotte was quivering with nervousness– the façade of being self- assured was an easy feat.

"Ms. Toutant has been invited to sit- in on the meeting," Nicholas announced as she rounded the large conference table.

Dean cleared his throat drawing the attention of the room in his direction. With all eyes on him, he smiled politely, but remained silent.

"Is there a problem, Mr. Proctor?" Nicholas asked unblinking, making focused eye contact with his subordinate.

"No sir, there's no problem at all," Dean answered looking away from him, suddenly uncomfortable.

"You're here," Nicholas Elliot beamed at Charlotte when she reached him. Standing, he pulled out the chair to his left. "Proctor, please continue."

"Oh. I . . . I . . . just feel that . . . I mean . . . sorry I lost track of what I was saying–"

"You were saying that readers are quickly losing interest in magazines due to the rise in demand of gossip sites streaming over the internet. However, research only proves your thesis partially. Statistics show that while mainstream entertainment is rapidly being channeled through technology, the trend of the avid reader is to always go back to the comfort of physically holding on to an actual book while reading. Hence, gaining information online verses through a tangible source is inconsistent. The issue isn't the portal in which the information is spread, rather the information itself. It's the material that we are producing that is the problem."

Dean snorted indignantly. "How does that apply for *Leisure Me Ready?* Most of our readers are 55 plus years old, and majority of them have little to *no experience* using a computer," he challenged. "If we were a fashion magazine, or a gossip channel what you're saying would be plausible, however–"

"However, even though our readers are not in that age bracket of being computer savvy our numbers are dropping drastically. Due to the recession people are retiring later, and those who are financially secure to retire don't feel comfortable squandering their money on frivolous activities," Charlotte stated boldly. "Our magazine focuses on the future retirement plans of the upper class, people who have thousands to spend, however, our economy isn't what it used to be and people are struggling. The same people who would have dropped thousands on a vacation in the middle of winter, now, would rather put the money aside for a rainy day."

"*Leisure Me Ready* brands leisure activities for senior citizens and individuals on the peak of retiring— it's our product . . . it's been our signature for two decades."

"Your point being what?" Charlotte asked, her big brown eyes regarding him carefully. "If people can't afford to take part in the leisure activities we are promoting our magazine isn't going to sell. Why buy a magazine which focuses solely on activities after retirement if you can't afford to take part in those activities?"

"If you're insinuating that we change—"

"I'm not insinuating, I'm clearly stating that there is always the option of exploring new ideas for content. People change, situations change, and time is not exempt . . . our audience is no longer interested. Whether it be from lack of income, or lack of interest in our marketable ideas— either way we're losing revenue. We need to spice things up a bit."

"I don't think—"

Nicholas raised his hand silencing Dean in mid- sentence. "Ms. Toutant may be on to something. Let's put it to a vote. All in favor of exploring the option of rebranding say, I."

Glancing around the table Charlotte smiled brightly at the unified support of her ideas from her colleagues.

"Well then there you have it. In the coming weeks I look forward to seeing what the advertising team puts together. If no one else had anything they would like to add . . . ?" he continued.

Silence.

"Well then meeting adjourned. Thank you all for your time. Ms. Toutant please stay behind for a moment."

Dean stood quickly, hurriedly gathering his belongings before rushing out of the conference room, his pride obviously bruised. Nicholas waited until the room was clear before he turned his attention to Charlotte who had been watching him, amused. Sitting on the edge of the wooden table Nicholas spun her chair closer toward him.

"You could have given me a heads up about the meeting. I had no idea what to expect," Charlotte glared at him.

"You think better on your feet," he shrugged. "It was better this way."

"Dean was annoyed that I was here."

"Dean's a prick. He has this weird superiority complex when it comes to women in the work place."

"I've noticed," she rolled her eyes. "Still, it probably wasn't a good idea to include me in the meeting. I'm not a board member, and I'm not a part of the sales team, so in all actuality there was no need for me to be here."

Narrowing his eyes, Nicholas thoughtfully rubbed the tip of his index finger along his jawline. "I wanted you here," he said finally. "And so you were."

Charlotte laughed. "It's that simple?"

"Pretty much," he answered, his laughter mirroring hers.

"You're going to make it worse."

"Make what worse?" he asked.

"The rumors, you're going to give people more to talk about if you don't stop showing me favoritism."

"Dimple, you're the Editor . . . it makes sense for you to be involved in a meeting with the board . . . don't worry so much."

Charlotte gave a half smile. "I thought I told you not to call me Dimple at work."

Nicholas shrugged nonchalantly. "We're the only ones in here," he smirked. "Do you seriously think people don't know that we're good friends by now? We're always together."

"Nick that's what I'm saying. People are watching us. We are like the talk of the office— it's uncomfortable."

"So are we not supposed to be friends at work? Should I ignore you?" he laughed entertained by her coyness.

"You find everything funny. I'm being serious right now."

Nicholas grinned, his dark grey eyes beaming at her. "Are you?" he mused, bringing his full bottom lip into his mouth.

Charlotte watched him through long lashes, her wandering gaze drifting, taking him all in. Friend or not, Nicholas was a very attractive man—a Prep boy by all standards, very clean cut. From his close shaved chestnut brown hair to his newly grown cinnamon goatee . . . he was gorgeous.

"You could at least wait until I'm not paying attention before you eye rape me," he teased.

His words caused a blush to set in her cheeks. "I don't know what you're talking about," Charlotte rolled her eyes, embarrassed.

"Mmhm."

"Just do me the favor of taking it easy at work. I don't want lies going around about me just because I'm friends with the boss."

"Fine. At work I'll treat you just like everyone else."

"That's all I ask."

"Well if you're done making your demands, get back to work."

"Sure thing, Chief," she smiled, rising from her chair and walking toward the exit. Turning around briefly she mouthed, "Thank you."

"You're welcome, Dimple."

Chapter Three

"I've changed my mind," Charlotte said apologetically. "I'm not going."

"What do you mean you're not going?" Patricia Foster demanded, sighing into the phone. "I thought we agreed that you would ignore any thoughts about cancelling, and just go for it?"

Patricia Foster, the Advertising Director for *Leisure Me Ready* magazine, and Charlotte's closest confidant was determined to accomplish her aspiration of setting up her introverted friend, and while she had thought that it was an ambition fought in vain, the notion of throwing in the towel seemed like an unforgivable inclination.

"I don't know Trish," Charlotte groaned. "The whole blind date thing is just too weird, you know?

Maybe, I'm just not ready to start dating . . . maybe it's too soon."

"Charlotte! We're not doing this again. There's always an excuse . . . just go on the date and see where it goes. You might be surprised."

"Or, I might end up dead and alone in Central Park," she grumbled, rolling her eyes at her friend's words. For months Charlotte had been quick on her feet, making up excuses at the last possible moment to get out of dates that her overzealous friend had adamantly arranged, and though she appreciated Patricia for caring as much as she had− at the same time she wished the other woman would cease in her feeble attempts at trying to play matchmaker.

"You won't end up dead and alone," Patricia laughed. "Trust me . . . would I ever put you in a dangerous situation?"

"Not intentionally," Charlotte mused.

"Not ever."

Heaving a sigh of frustration, Charlotte pouted her lips in deep contemplation. *I really don't have much to lose . . . right? I mean what's the worst that could happen, well other than this dude being a total psycho and me dying at the tender age of twenty eight?*

"Hello? Charlotte? Are you there?" Patricia shouted into the phone. "Did you hang up?"

"I'm here."

"Get dressed. He'll be waiting for you in front of Keairs on Broadway at nine."

"What's his phone number?"

Patricia laughed softly in her ear. "There's no way I'm trusting you with that information."

"What? How will I call him when I'm close by?" Charlotte demanded.

"Girly, who are you trying to fool. I know your games, as soon as I give you his number you'll be calling with an excuse to reschedule—"

"That's not true."

"It's the God honest truth, and you know it. You'll come up with something that no one thinks to question . . . you're running a fever . . . you were called back into work . . . your dog has fallen ill."

"I don't have a dog," Charlotte said unamused.

"You'll make one up," Patricia declared. "And to stop that timeless debacle from reoccurring I'm only telling you need to know information."

"Are you insane? You're sending me out to meet a strange man at nine o' clock at night by myself all the while refusing to give me information about this person."

"He's single, in his thirties, and childless. Everything else is learnable through conversation."

She really is insane, Charlotte thought. "If you think that I'm stepping foot outside my door to meet someone who I barely know anything about, you're mistaken. Do me the solace and cancel for me. Good night."

"Alright. Alright. His name is Jeremy Brooks, and he's a friend of a friend. Charlotte, this guy is a catch, and if you don't show up tonight he'll be standing out in the cold waiting for you in front of Keairs for God knows how long because I' am not canceling."

"Patricia."

"Charlotte. I'm not joking. I' am not going to call him and cancel. If you want to cancel . . . show up and do it in person."

"That makes absolutely no sense."

"And neither does the thought of a beautiful woman in her twenties sitting around in her apartment when there is such a big world outside her window waiting to be explored," Patricia snarked.

Charlotte smacked her lips loudly into the phone. "Fine," she huffed. "Okay, fine. I'll meet him, but only to tell him that I'm not interested and then I'm leaving.

"Do what you have to do," Patricia said non-phased. "All I ask is that you show up."

***

Stepping out of her apartment building Charlotte tucked her hands into her coat pocket grateful that she had opted to wear her infinity scarf. Inhaling the cold November morning air she closed her eyes smiling as the early wintry rush spread through her body. Walking quickly in the direction of the subway she glanced down at her watch. *6:43 a.m. Crap. I can't believe that I over slept,* she grimaced. Running across the street Charlotte flagged down a cab quickly jumping into the backseat before anyone else had a chance to do so. Smiling to herself, she felt a quiet sense of pride that a county girl from Baltimore had mastered the art of hailing down a cab so effectively in the busy streets of New York.

"Tompkins Square Park, Avenue B, please," she said once inside.

"Yes, ma' am."

Charlotte squinted her eyes in the darkness of the cab in hopes of getting a good look at the driver, but to no avail. Shrugging her shoulders in defeat she leaned back into the hard black cushion and rested her head against the seat.

"How are you this morning?" she asked the cab driver.

"I'm well, Ms. How are you?"

Charlotte smiled at the stranger's heavy Indian accent. "A bit tired. I had a long night."

"Oh. Uh, I'm sorry to hear that. Many hopes that you receive plenty of rest this evening Ms."

"Thank you," she yawned, closing her eyes. "Can you let me know when we get there?" she mumbled.

"I'm sorry, Ms.?" The driver frowned in a state of confusion. "What is it that you want?"

Opening her eyes she blinked several times in an attempt to stay awake. "Don't mind me," Charlotte said staring out of the stained window at the hundreds of people walking the streets in the early morning hours. The fast pace of the Big City still amazed her. It was as if the streets themselves pulsed with an undying energy. "Don't mind me at all," she repeated her voice barely a whisper as she allowed her eyes to close once more.

Chapter Four

Walking through the foyer Charlotte avoided the watchful eyes of her gossiping co- workers. Pretending to be engrossed in her planner, she skimmed her fingers over blank pages in hopes to deter the small talk of the catty secretaries. Although she had grown use to the many rumors that were floating around about her supposed affair with Nicholas, she hated the uncomfortable feeling of knowing that she would be the subject of interest whenever she passed.

"Good morning Ms. Toutant," called a familiar voice from behind her. "Do you have a moment?"

Charlotte turned around quickly, eyeing Nicholas quizzically. "Yes, sir. What can I help you with?" she screeched rather loudly, aiming to get the attention of the idle chatterboxes.

Nicholas furrowed his brows as he eyed her curiously. "Are you okay?" he asked, closing the space between them.

"Yes sir. I'm well, thank you. What can I do for you, sir?" she responded taking a step away from him.

Biting his lower lip, Nicholas narrowed his eyes at Charlotte, confusion evident in his piercing grey eyes.

"What can I help you with, sir?" she continued, hoping that their audience was paying close attention.

"What are you doing?" he asked, perplexed.

Pleading with her eyes, Charlotte nodded in the direction of the gathering onlookers. This was their golden opportunity to showcase their strictly platonic business relationship. "Please," she mouthed.

Combing his long fingers through his goatee Nicholas contemplated her request. "You're late. Patricia mentioned that you were up late gathering research for a *new project*."

"Did she?" Charlotte frowned.

"She did. I'm curious as to how your findings panned out," he grinned. "After all, if this *project* was worth you losing sleep over . . . I think it's only right that I learn more about it."

Charlotte regarded him closely, but remained silent. He was baiting her, and she didn't like it. Licking her lips in deep deliberation she inched closer to Nicholas. "What happened to you treating me like a regular employee?" she whispered.

Nicholas laughed softly. Placing his hand on the arch of her lower back he pulled her into him, ignoring the gasping sounds of the women who had gathered behind the receptionist desk to the left of them. "What happened to us not keeping things from one another?" he breathed into her ear. His lips brushing against her lobe causing a shiver to stir in the pit of her stomach.

Charlotte opened her mouth to speak, but decided against it knowing that she would regret her words as soon as she had said them. Turning away from Nicholas she hurried in the direction of the elevators feeling frustrated. *Jerk!* She scoffed annoyed by his gull. *There goes trying to banish the*

idea that our relationship is strictly professional.
"Great," she sighed under her breath.

***

The atmosphere in the conference room appeared solemn at best as Nicholas handed each of his employees a stack of thick manila folders. Raising one in the air he said, "This unfortunately is our last hope at trying to find a life line within the framework of our magazine marque, we have forty- eight hours to get our hands on something worth preserving. Hayward Fissicle, the owner of *Gizzelle Bridal* has bought a share of *Leisure Me Ready*, a substantial share, making him a highly beneficial board member."

"That could work to our benefit," Patricia offered as she opened the folder with certain fingers.

"How so?" Nicholas asked.

"Well, your father and Fissicle have worked together on different takeovers in the past. I'm sure if you gave him a call . . . ."

Nicholas mused over the thought before shaking his head adamantly. "No, that wouldn't work. Family and business are two separate entities."

"Nicholas, if Fissicle is a part of your father's circle I don't see a reason for you not to use that to your advantage. Ask your father to speak to him about keeping *Leisure Me Ready* afoot. He very well may appreciate the idea of helping out his friend's son."

Staring into the concerned faces of his team, he appeared to be vexed. Agitated, Nicholas combed his fingers through his hair. While his father was a key factor in his businesslike developmental growth, he had never used the benefit of having a business savvy father to his advantage. In all honesty, he preferred to seek and accomplish success by his own means, and by his own standards. "I'm not interested in involving my father into this situation," he said matter- of- factly, his tone stern.

"Patricia does have a point," Dean challenged, looking around the table he encouraged others to agree with him. "Your father's involvement could be the last chance we have at not being taken over by Fissicle's company."

"Did you not hear what I just said? Nicholas demanded. "Fissicle has already bought a substantial share of the company, and is now a member of the board . . . he has *already* taken over. The issue is the uncertainty of whether or not he plans on dislodging our team to bring in members of his own, or if he even plans on keeping the magazine afloat."

"Take away his opportunity in making a conscious decision. Have your father speak to him," Dean pushed.

Nicholas stared at the other man shrewdly. "That's not an option."

Dean groaned indignantly. "This is crap."

"Excuse me?"

"The whole spiel about family and business being two separate entities . . . what about business and pleasure?" Dean snorted. "You don't seem to mind mixing those two ordinances."

"Oh crap," Patricia muttered quietly. "It's about to get real."

Nicholas squared his shoulders, furrowing his brows as he spoke. "What exactly is that supposed to mean?"

"You know as well as everyone else sitting at this table what it means. You called a team meeting . . . and we're all here with the exception of one. Charlotte seems to be among the missing, and I'm sure that's fine by you, right. She can pretty much do whatever it is she wants . . . show up to meetings that she isn't a part of, strut into work late, leave early, miss meetings, and yet she is still employed. Obviously, there are lines that have been crossed as far as you and Ms. Toutant are concerned, so I guess what I'm asking Chief is why not take one for the *team* and cross just one more. Certainly considering what's at risk for the staff that has worked so hard for you over the years—"

"That's enough," Nicholas snapped.

"If you would just—"

Slamming his fists onto the hard cherry oak table, he regarded Dean intently, his grey eyes a molten steel. "I said, that's enough," he shouted, causing Barbara, the robust Latina woman sitting closest to him to jump. "My father is not taking part in any functions of this company whether they are successes or failures; he has no part to play in either. And as far as my relationship with Ms. Toutant– it's not now, nor will it ever be any of your business. She carries her weight around here, and that's all you need to concern yourself with as far as she is concerned. Got it?"

Dean stared at Nicholas, his mouth agape as if he were about to argue but opted in remaining silent.

"I asked you a question," Nicholas snarked, unsatisfied.

"Got it. Boss."

"Good. As for the rest of you, forty- eight hours. Make me proud."

Chapter Five

Charlotte lay on her chaise lounge wrapped in a gold faux blanket slowly drifting off to sleep as the voices of Dorothy and Auntie Em caressed her sub- consciousness. It was a Toutant family tradition to watch *The Wizard of Oz* at least once on Thanksgiving, once being the operative word, Charlotte could vastly recall years of watching the classic more than a few times in one sitting. Snuggling into the plush of her coverlet she allowed her mind to drift off to thoughts of years past. She missed her family, her friends, Baltimore. And while she found the ability to turn off the switch to her past beneficial, there were times when she couldn't help but take a stroll down memory lane. Thoughts of her parents, Babet and Manuel, of her kid sister, Adeline rayed through her consciousness. Visions of laughter and love clouded her mind causing a soft smile to form at her lips. She couldn't help but wonder how they were spending their holiday, if her father had chased her mother around with the turkey's drumstick, if her mother had spent most of the morning screaming for Adeline to turn down her music. Had their next door neighbor stopped by at wee hours of the morning asking for Manuel's homemade JuJu sauce, a Creole family recipe that had been passed on through the generations. Charlotte's mouth watered at the thought of her father's sauce. For as long as she could remember her mother had asked for the ingredients, but to no avail, her father was intent on keeping his secrets. Secrets. *My family and their secrets,* she cringed.

    Without warning the happiness of her former relationships with individuals she had loved her entire life was overcast by reality. The transgressions of her other sibling quickly making its presence known; the foundation of everything she had believed in was broken. Marguerite, her most beloved sister, had proven that blood was not a means for loyalty and respect, but in fact that family was the pretense of love and expectations that were not always met. After all, she did not expect to catch her fiancé in bed with her sister, nor did she expect for her parents to know about the affair— but that was the funny thing about expectations, they always seemed to run parallel to what was seemingly expected.

Charlotte opened her eyes in the darkness of her living room, hating the moisture that coated her cheeks but refusing to wipe away the effects of being betrayed. Her tears were hot, matching her disposition on matters of the heart. Pushing the memory of her sister's disloyalty into the back of her mind did not aid in the process of forgiveness. "Get it together, Charlotte," she chastised herself, hating the direction her thoughts had taken. Closing her eyes once more she pulled the blanket over her head hoping the darkness would work as an aid in her attempt at falling asleep. Being unconscious is exactly what she needed; at least then her mind would have peace. Drowsiness had just begun to settle in when a loud thumping sounded outside of her apartment door. Glancing at the digital clock that sat front face on her television mantle, she frowned. *7:23p.m.*

"Who is it?" Charlotte called, making her way to the door, huffing as she tightened the blanket around her thin frame.

"He who bears gifts," answered a familiar masculine voice.

Nicholas? What is he doing here? She wondered. Opening the door she gasped at the sight of him. A bright smile reached his mercury grey eyes as she stared at him thoughtfully.

"Are you going to let me in?" he asked, feigning a look of annoyance. "This is kinda' heavy," he said, nodding at the silver containers in his large hands.

Charlotte glanced at the food filled basins and then back at him, her frown deepening. "What is all of this?" she asked, stepping aside to allow him entry into her home.

"What does it look like?"

"I don't know . . . left overs?" she mused.

"That's a bit tacky."

"Bringing leftovers? I never thought of that as being tacky, but then again we are from different social classes, after all . . . ."

"After all," he smiled. "Anyway I knew you'd be home, alone, hungry, moping, and feeling sorry for yourself . . . I thought the least I could do was bring by something to eat."

"Is it catered?"

"The best food is," Nicholas laughed. "I got the basics, Mac-n- Cheese, Sweet Potatoes, Shredded Turkey, Collard Greens, Stuffing, and for Dessert Apple Pie and Banana Pudding."

"Wow. You went all out," she beamed at him. The familiar aroma of the seasonal food caused a sweet ache to form on the inside. It wasn't until that moment that she realized how hungry she truly was. Walking swiftly past him Charlotte quickly made her way into the kitchen where she hurriedly searched for plates and eating utensils. *I know there should be at least two clean forks,* she groaned inwardly suddenly annoyed by her house keeping skills, or lack thereof for that matter.

"You okay in there?" he called at the sound of cabinets slamming behind him.

"I need another fork," she sighed. "Give me a sec–"

Nicholas laughed. "I have plastic forks, and plates' right here."

"You thought of everything," Charlotte smiled appreciatively. "Thank you," she said, taking a seat beside him on the couch.

"Not much to think of . . . I scarcely remember a time when you didn't have to wash dishes before we could eat," he shrugged.

"Jerk."

"I'm being honest," he chuckled.

"And a jerk."

Ignoring her sentiment Nicholas took his time opening the aluminum containers careful not to get burned by the steam.

"Not that I'm complaining, but what are you doing here? I thought you were headed to Cape Cod with your family for Thanksgiving?" she asked, licking her lips as she piled Sweet Potatoes onto her plate.

"Something came up," he shrugged, not bothering to explain himself.

Charlotte glowered. "Oh. Is everything okay?" she probed, a look of concern in her chestnut brown eyes.

"Yeah, it's nothing like that. I just didn't make the trip this year . . . and good thing I didn't, otherwise you'd be sitting here hungry and alone," he mused.

Charlotte felt reprimanded by his words, but decided to take his acknowledgement for what it was; after all, his assessment of the situation wasn't completely wrong. Before he had arrived, she was indeed hungry and alone.

"So, am I forgiven?" he asked after a moment's silence.

"Forgiven? For what?"

"Refusing to pretend that you're my subordinate and nothing more . . . ."

"About that?" Charlotte furrowed her arched brows showcasing her confusion over the matter. "I thought we had an understanding?"

"Dimple, I'm not going to pretend that you're just my employee. Besides, I'm not that good of an actor anyway, even if I tried to keep my distance from you someone would make assumptions about the lack of attention I'm giving you . . . people need something to talk about, and unfortunately it just so happens that the people we work with find gossiping about us to be most entertaining."

"Even still, as my best friend the least you could have done was attempt to play along."

Nicholas rubbed his index finger along his chiseled jawline, teasing the dark hair that covered his face. "Does it really mean that much to you? Putting on the façade that our relationship is strictly professional?" he asked, gazing at her deeply.

"Yes, it does. I don't want to be ridiculed at work . . . I want to be respected for all that I do, not because people think I'm doing you, no pun intended," she snorted.

Nicholas smiled broadly at her. "If you say so," he laughed. "Fine . . . fine. From now on you're my employee and nothing more while we're in the workplace. You have my word."

"You said that before, and look what happened," she argued.

Nicholas shrugged. "Well this time I mean it."

Jerk.

***

Charlotte stretched her long torso before opening her eyes, slightly confused when she realized that she was still in the living room. Blinking rapidly, she squinted as her eyes adjusted to the bright autumn sun that shined through her snow white curtains. Glancing at the mantle clock she smiled. *8:00 a.m. and nowhere to go,* she thought, overjoyed. While everyone was out fighting the hustle and bustle of Black Friday shopping she was content with the notion of staying inside to enjoy the benefits of online bargaining. Turning onto her side, she tossed the cover off of her thin body stretching again as she stared down at Nicholas who had made a bed out of throw pillows and an old quilted comforter her mother had crotched for her years ago.

She wasn't surprised that he had spent the night, after all it had become a custom of theirs to stay up until early morning hours watching movies, and talking until they eventually fell asleep. Throwing her legs over the couch she stood in front of him, a small smile playing at her lips at the sight of him lying there so peacefully; it was a rare sight to be seen. Stress from the magazine came in torrents, having to make difficult decisions in regards to the future employment of his staff was overwhelming and had started to take a toll on him. More often than not he was consumed with thoughts of business unable to focus on anything beyond budgets and briefs.

Inching away from him Charlotte tiptoed into the kitchen careful not to make noise as she opened the refrigerator, pulling out a carton of eggs, and a half used stick of butter. "Clean pans, clean pans . . . ." she whispered, hoping to find at least one that she didn't have to wash. "Sweet," she cooed, sighting one behind a set of plastic plates. Turning on the electric stove she placed the pan onto the red lit surface not wasting time in cutting two thin pieces of the salted coating into the heated pan. Opening the refrigerator once more she grabbed three potatoes, and reaching for the cutting board on the counter space opposite the stove she kicked the cold box closed, silently making her way around the small kitchen with a purpose. After all that he had done for her the night before the least she could do was make him breakfast, even if it wasn't much.

***

The smell of sunny side up eggs and fried potatoes filled her petite apartment causing Nicholas to stir in his sleep. Swallowing hard he turned onto his side flexing his back muscles as he did so. The fatigued feeling that exhaustion introduced made the floor a welcoming divan, however, now that energy was no longer lacking, the hardness of the wooden surface had proven unpleasant.

Nicholas remained under the comfort of the homely quilt as his bright eyes gazed around the living room. He was alone. Leaning on his elbows, he turned his head in the direction of the kitchen, frowning when he saw that Charlotte was nowhere in sight. He moved then, suddenly rising to his feet he made his way down the carpeted hallway to her bedroom.

"Dimple," he called as he knocked with the knuckle of his index finger. "Are you in here?"

Answered with silence, Nicholas pushed open the door without hesitation, walking into the all-white room with a faint smile on his lips. It amazed him how neat of a person Charlotte was— everything had a place, and nothing was ever out of position. There was an even amount of pillows that lined her bed, a pair of candles on her bedside table, two books on her bed nook— their titles facing forward, two plants on either side of her dresser, and two tall lamp stands on adjacent walls center-piecing her suede loveseat. Shaking his head, he stood confounded at the thought of how a person could display major signs of OCD by means of one area of their home, but lack the necessity of being compulsive in other areas, hence the kitchen which was always in disarray.

"What are you doing?" Charlotte asked from behind him, a curious grin on her glistening face.

Nicholas turned at the sound of her voice. Shrugging his shoulders he smiled at her. "Looking for you. Where were you?"

"I went for a run. I left you a note . . . it's next to your breakfast."

"Oh," Nicholas took a step in Charlotte's direction his eyes never leaving hers. "How was your run?" he asked, tucking a stray strand of hair behind her ear.

"Amazing, I love the crisp New York air," she beamed. "It's so refreshing."

"Thank you for breakfast, you're too kind," he laughed softly.

Charlotte's eyes beamed at him delightedly, her face flushed red as she tried to suppress a smile. "I know. I know," she chuckled, "I' am pretty wonderful."

"Yeah you are," he said, sharing in her laughter. "But the test is whether or not it's appetizing, taste is everything."

"Oh?" she teased. "Is taste everything?"

Nicholas narrowed his eyes at her, a boyish smile teasing his lips. "Absolutely."

"Then come," she said, pulling him out of her bedroom. "Let's see if your *taste* is the same as mine."

Nicholas licked his lips holding back the first words that came to mind, intent on keeping his thoughts to himself, he answered, "Let's."

Chapter Six

DECEMBER 2008

"I knew this would happen," Dean grumbled. "I called it months ago. Fissicle has no intention of keeping *Leisure Me Ready* in business. It has been his agenda from the very beginning to integrate his employees into the company before blindsiding us."

"Calm down," Nicholas ordered, rubbing his temples in agitation.

"How am I supposed to calm down knowing that any day, at any hour I could be out of a job? I've been with this magazine for five years now, and just like that," Dean snapped his fingers, "It's all over."

"Are we really going to lose our jobs?" squeaked Rebecca, the Budget Analyst.

"No one is going to lose their job," Nicholas assured Rebecca, and the full room of weary employees. Glaring at Dean disdainfully Nicholas rose from his seat at the head of the conference table. "Listen, I understand your concerns, and I can only imagine how worried you all must feel right now— But you have to trust that I would never allow any members of my team to be left without employment. Now with that being said I have some news . . . this morning I had a meeting with Fissicle, and he has agreed to keep all of *our* staff on payroll. However, certain departments have been deemed unnecessary, and unfortunately if you're contracted under those specific teams you'll have one of two options. The first involves taking a pay cut to keep that faction afloat, or moving to a different department where it is very possible that there will be a pay cut congruent on an individuals' skills and education."

"Are you serious?" Dean laughed sardonically. "So exactly what departments were put up to fry in this nightmare?"

"The list will be posted within the next forty-eight hours," Nicholas said, regarding the other man coldly.

"This is such utter crap!" Dean continued. "If only you would have asked your father to speak to the man we wouldn't—"

"We would be in the same situation. Fissicle is not interested in a retirement magazine. Let's face it folks, even if we weren't bought out by Fissicle it wouldn't have been a long road for us to travel. Our sales have been down for some time now. The economy isn't what it used to be and people are retiring later and later as the years' progress. And when they finally do have the opportunity to consider retirement more often than not their incomes are barely enough to keep their households in order. I hate that it happened this way, but believe me when I say that this outcome was inevitable. Now, the idea of a Wedding Magazine didn't seem all too appealing to me at first either, but the numbers are remarkable. With the general sales alone everyone at this table will be satisfied with the pay raises, and yearly bonuses in due time– just stick with me, and I promise you will not regret it," Nicholas said assuring the large group in front of him, but his molten gaze was focused on Charlotte's almond browns.

"Let me ask you something?" Dean pressed, tearing Nicholas' attention away from the woman sitting a few chairs away from him. "While we are taking these pay cuts, and awaiting the promises you have in store for us– what is happening with your salary?"

"Excuse me?"

"How will your wages be affected by this take over?" Dean demanded not cutting any cards.

Nicholas stared at his employee squarely, mentally counting backwards as he prayed for patience.

"Mr. Elliot is Editor- and- Chief, of course his pay should remain the same regardless of who owns shares, or the change in company advertising. As long as he holds the position as lead in command he should get paid as such. His salary is not interchangeable to ours," Charlotte glanced around the room as she spoke. "He's already explained that there was nothing else that could have been done. We've known about the take over for almost a month now, and in knowing such we knew that there was a possibility that Fissicle would backdoor *Leisure Me Ready* for the sole benefit of *Gizzelle Bridal*. It's already done, now let's move on."

"Funny . . . You referring to him as Mr. Elliot . . . forgive me for prying, but are you that formal when the two of you are alone?"

"Dean," Nicholas warned.

"Charlotte?" Dean insisted, ignoring Nicholas' threatening tone. "I'm sure that I'm not the only one here that's interested in the dynamic of your relationship with the *Editor and Chief*, so, when he's screwing your brains out are you still so formal, or are you on a first name basis?"

"Dean! That's enough!" Patricia chastised.

"I'm sorry Patricia, but this is a joke. I can guarantee that this man will negotiate a way for Charlotte to keep her salary while the rest of us are forced to put on a happy face."

"I am treated no differently than anyone in this room," Charlotte defended. "You are out of line, Dean."

While her demeanor was calm on the outside, on the inside she was screaming, outraged by the nerve, by the un-blegigated gull of the man. Tears gathered in her eyes, but she refused to let them fall. She wouldn't give him the satisfaction of knowing that his words had cut her.

"Dean, please excuse yourself," Nicholas ordered, his tone barely above an octave. There was heat in his words, an inferno that was slowly building.

"Is the meeting adjourned?" the man asked mockingly. "I couldn't think of anything better than to excuse myself from this room."

Nicholas snorted indignantly, "From the building, Dean, excuse yourself from the building, and leave your security badge with Patricia on your way out."

"What?" Dean shouted, his face a grotesque mask. "You can't fire me! You have no grounds for my termination. I'm superior at my job. Fissicle–"

"Could careless who I fire, or hire as long as he's making a profit, and Fissicle aside, I am Editor and Chief and what I say goes— end of story. Now get out."

An uncomfortable silence filled the room as Dean rose from his chair. Snatching the badge from around his neck he struggled to control his breathing. "I will fight you on this," he promised, throwing the plastic badge on the table as he passed Patricia. "You're going to regret this!"

Charlotte grimaced as Dean made his way past her, eyeing her hatefully, before walking to the large wooden doors and forcefully pushing them open as he exited the room.

"Any questions, comments, or concerns?" Nicholas asked, backing away from the large rectangular table.

Silence.

"None?" he pressed.

Silence.

"Well then get back to work."

Chapter Seven

The weeks that followed the takeover came and went with little hindrance as everyone fell in unison supporting their fellow staff members with the various positions and responsibilities that came along with their new contract. Charlotte had spent more time than she wished to admit studying the outlines of past accounts hoping that in time she would be able to emulate the skills of Hayward Fissicle's current employees. By the looks of prior documents it was quite clear that their new shareholder liked things done in a particular manner, from the technique of filing briefs to the never ending documentation of client based conversations— the man was a stickler for systematization. And while she had total trust in

Nicholas and his promise to not leave any of his staff blindsided, Charlotte couldn't help but feel concerned at the possibility of Fissicle laying off the *Leisure Me Ready* stragglers who hadn't been able to keep pace with the fast moving bridal magazine.

Staring at her reflection in the full length closet mirror Charlotte adjusted her cashmere sweater, turning this way and that as she harshly judged the reflection gazing back at her. With her heeled leather boots on she stood at 5'7, the stilettos adding a good three inches to her petite height of 5'4, and while she typically felt comfortable wearing high heels a sudden ray of insecurities had begun to settle in. Making plans with Jeremy for an evening out on the town had seemed like a romantic fourth date, but as the hour drew nearer the idea of getting dolled up to impress someone she barely knew felt like a total waste of time. *If I wear heels I'll be taller than him, but flats look terrible with these jeans . . . it's not like he's that short,* she sighed inwardly. *If anything I could walk a few inches away from him so that no one would notice . . . .*

Shrugging, she turned off the light to her walk in closet before quickly making her way through her un-kept apartment. Grabbing her purse and keys off of the corner wall table Charlotte wrestled with the idea of canceling. Silently, she wondered if the process was worth all of the stress, picking out the *right* shoes, the *right* outfit . . . it all seemed so silly, so mundane. "No man is worth that much effort," she mumbled aloud allowing the locked door to slam shut behind her.

Chapter Eight

Charlotte struggled to keep her eyes open as she fumbled for her keys in the dim lit hallway. The night hadn't been a total disaster. Walking through the streets of Manhattan was *nice,* the light meal shared between the two of them was *nice,* as was the night cap at his apartment. Still, from the moment she saw him standing by the light pole in front of the corner bakery on 8th street, she couldn't help but want to be elsewhere.

Stepping into her flat Charlotte blanked rapidly, squinting several times in an attempt to adjust her eyes to the darkness. *I thought I turned on the living room lamp before I left*, she thought, dropping her purse and keys on the wall table console before making her way down the long hallway that led to the kitchen. Flipping on the light switch, she gasped, taken aback at the cleanliness of the place. Pots and pans lay flat on her counter space drying while utensils filled her dish strainer pointing this way and that as water dripped off of them. The smell of lemon and pine filled her senses causing her nose to twitch subtly. With a faint smile on her lips Charlotte sauntered into the living room, removing her shoes as she did so, dropping them along the way. Turning the corner she paused at the end of the couch, tilting her head as she stared down at the man she had grown so fond of in the short time they had known one another. Although it had only been two years since they had had their first encounter it seemed like an eternity ago, somehow he had become her closest confidant— the only person she felt she could truly depend on. Without thought she turned on the end table lamp, folding her arms across her chest as she sat on the shoulder of the couch, crossing her legs in front of her.

Nicholas twisted his face, squeezing his eyes shut in protest to the sudden brightness of the room. "Turn off the light," he complained, covering his face with his forearm.

"Breaking and entering again I see . . . it would be nice if you called to give me the heads up that you're coming over."

"It's not breaking in if I used a key," he sighed, turning away from the brightness emanating from the lamp.

"You only have permission to use that key in case of emergencies . . . was there an emergency that I didn't know about?" she teased, leaning forward allowing her body to rest against his.

Nicholas adjusted his frame under hers, turning so that their faces were only inches apart. Narrowing his greys, he watched her carefully—their sudden closeness causing a curious sensation to start in the pit of his stomach, the feeling was one that he wasn't quite accustomed to. "How was your date?" he asked, breaking the silence that stretched on between them.

Charlotte gazed down at him lost in the bottomless pool of silver, his full lips, and unruly chestnut brown hair. *God, he's gorgeous,* she sighed inwardly, fighting to keep those lurking thoughts at bay. *Charlotte, quit it!* She admonished herself, frustrated, that the notion of his looks had even become a factor. *Don't be messy . . . he's your best friend . . . don't be messy.*

"Dimple?" he whispered, tucking stray hairs behind her ears, his expression unreadable. "What are you thinking about?"

"Nothing worth mentioning," she shrugged, leaning away from him. "Thanks for washing the dishes," she smiled, wanting nothing more than to change the direction of their conversation.

Nicholas furrowed his brows, confusion paramount. "Not a problem."

"I'm going to call it a night . . . I'm exhausted."

"Is that your way of asking me to leave?" he asked, dismayed by the sudden change in her demeanor.

"Nicholas, you know that you're always welcomed to stay," she sighed. "I'm just . . . tired."

He moved then. Pulling her back toward him, Nicholas asked, "Is that all? You're just tired?"

"Yes," she lied, her voice barely above a whisper.

With one hand on either side of her face Nicholas tilted Charlotte's head back forcing her to look into his deep greys. Blinking rapidly, she attempted to turn her head needing to break the contact, but her effort was in vain, his vice like grip was too strong to sway. Gazing into his molten mercury eyes she felt like she was falling forward, fast and hard.

"Are you sure?" he pressed, narrowing his eyes at her.

"Yes."

". . . okay. "I'll see you tomorrow," he said, releasing her from his hold, his stare never wavering. "Sweet dreams," he mumbled, kissing the top of her head before backing away from her. Standing, Nicholas rounded the couch and headed for the door.

"Don't leave," Charlotte said suddenly, feeling abashed by the neediness in her tone.

Turning to face her once more Nicholas frowned as his piercing greys regarded her intently. "You just said—"

"Just stay," she shrugged apologetically. Her thoughts were all over the place as were her feelings and while she hated not being able to explain either to Nicholas, she felt that omission was necessary until she had clear reign over what she was feeling toward him. The out of sight, out of mind approach worked well. When she was free from the temptation of his scent, his demeanor, his charm— the thought of Nicholas as anything other than her best friend seemed aberrant. However, when he was standing so close, the heat of his body, the hunted smell of his cologne, the way he looked at her— there was an unspoken chemistry that forced her to see him beyond the means of friendship, in those moments he was a man, and she was a woman— and in her mind those thin lines became easily blurred.

"I'll stay if you tell me what's wrong."

"Nothing's—"

"Dimple . . . what's wrong?"

"I just," she shook her head in defeat, looking away from him seemingly embarrassed. "Um. I just . . . I–"

The sudden sound of chiming bells caught Charlotte's attention, causing her to jump. *Saved by the bell . . . literally*, she thought as she walked into the dining room where her cell phone had been laying idly on the small oak table.

"Dimple," he called after her. "Are you seriously going to answer the phone right now?"

"It might be an important call," she answered lamely, turning away from him. She was a coward. It was that simple. A coward who wasn't above being honest with herself, and honestly, she was grateful for the interruption.

"And this isn't important?" Nicholas asked, exasperated.

Grabbing hold of the device, she glowered. *One missed call- unknown number.* Dialing -1 she brought the phone to her ear, her face contorting into a broken mask at the sound of her mother's voice.

Charli . . . it's mom. Daddy's sick . . . and he's asking for you. He needs you here . . . we all do. Please come home sweetie. I love you . . . .

Charlotte dropped her phone unable to maintain a steady grip on the object that had transferred the life shattering news. *My dad's sick . . . is he dying? He can't be dying, right? God wouldn't let him die . . . would he?* Covering her wet face with shaking hands, Charlotte fell to her knees ignoring the sting of the carpet on her forearms. Nicholas was by her side at once, instantly pulling her into him, his arms wrapped tightly around her quivering body.

"What happened?" he demanded. "What's wrong?"

"My dad," she cried, unable to speak the words aloud. "My dad."

Chapter Nine

The dark skies of the early morning hours slowly transformed into an array of colorful hues as dawn made its presence known. Charlotte shifted in the passenger seat opening her eyes to catch glimpses of Nicholas. His expression was a serious one as he stared at the long road ahead of him. Stretching in the confined space Charlotte rolled down the window thankful for the bitter breeze that blew into the cream Chrysler 300. They were still on I-95; it felt like they would never make it off the highway. It was by far the longest 195 miles she would ever have to travel.

"You're hot?" Nicholas asked, turning the nozzle toward him, lowering the temperature of the heat that was jetting out at full speed.

"Heat makes me sleepy . . . I want to stay awake," she answered, her voice barely above an octave. Fear overrode her thoughts, making it impossible for her to focus on anything other than the image of her once vigorous father lying stiffly on his back, unable to perform the daily routines that people in good health generally take for granted.

"If you're tired, sleep," he ordered.

"I'm fine. Let's talk . . . distract me."

Nicholas rested the back of his head against the seat in deep contemplation. There was plenty on his mind, but the solemn mood brought on by the unraveling of unfortunate events gave him reason to pause. Feeling restless, Charlotte groaned aloud, roughly combing her fingers through her hair. The silence was deafening as the feeling of dread consumed her. She needed something, anything, to be a haven of absolute distraction.

"Call your mom," Nicholas said after a while, making quick glances at her as he changed lanes.

Charlotte shook her head adamantly. "No." She hadn't called her mother in a little over two years, and she didn't need to make an exception. "We'll be in Baltimore in less than an hour. I'll find out what's going on then."

"Calling her would take away unnecessary anxiety, and at least then you'd know exactly what's going on with your father."

"I said, no, now would you drop it," she snapped.

Nicholas nodded, but didn't respond. Merging into the far left lane he readjusted his weight in the seat trying to get comfortable. Out of the corner of his eye he watched as Charlotte stared blankly out the window. Every part of his being yearned to reach out and touch her, to comfort her, but he knew that she would pull away from him, that she would reject the solace offered in the protection of his arms. There was a hard-ness about her that he never fully understood, like a shell that wouldn't submit to the idea of being cracked she was unbelievably introverted, giving nothing away, yet drawing him into her as if he were under a spell.

"Nicholas?" she whispered, breaking him from his thoughts. "I'm sorry. I had no right to yell at you . . . I know that you're only trying to help."

"It's okay," he said seemingly un-phased by her temper. "You're forgiven."

Charlotte smiled briefly, the expression faltering before it reached her eyes. "Am I?"

"Always."

"Nicholas?"

"Dimple?"

"About earlier . . . at my place . . . I don't want you to—"

"I almost forgot. Fissicle stopped by my office today," Nicholas said suddenly, interrupting her. "He dropped off a few promotional gifts." Nicholas knew where their conversation was headed and in that moment that particular conversation wasn't one to be had. As far as he was concerned she had had enough on her mind, and everything else could wait.

"Oh?"

"Look in my duffle bag."

Charlotte turned in her seat stretching her torso backward in search for the travel bags that lined the car floor. *Is this it?* She wondered, pulling on the first heavy bag she could reach. Squeezing the sack through the small space of the front seats, she sat it on her lap, wasting little time opening the large carrier, careful not to snag his clothes with the zipper. "What exactly am I looking for?"

"You'll see it."

"How many outfits did you pack?" she laughed in spite of herself as she looked through his luggage.

"When traveling you can never be too prepared," Nicholas replied, his laughter an imitation of hers.

Charlotte bit her lip at the sight of a ring box under his perfectly folded cardigans. "What's this?" she asked dumbly.

"What does it look like? Open it."

Charlotte opened the small square box exposing a sky blue topaz diamond. "A ring," she gasped, taking it from the safety of its box. "Can I try it on?"

Nicholas nodded his approval at her request.

"It's my size."

"Do you like it?"

"Are you serious?" she choked, amazed at how it shined. "I love it. Fissicle gave this to you?"

"Amongst other things. The magazine is advertising this ring as our feature for the month of January."

"And so he just gave it to you? The price of this ring is probably more than what I make in a month." When he didn't respond she probed, "How much is it? Two thousand? Three?" Charlotte guessed, happy for the sudden distraction.

"Seven," he said, his tone impassive.

"Seven thousand dollars! There is seven thousand dollars on my finger right now?" she gushed. "And he just gave it to you? Just like that, he handed you a seven thousand dollar ring, for free?" The idea of it all was too insane for her to fathom. "Rich people do the craziest things."

Nicholas chuckled at her giddiness over something so small. "Keep it."

"What?"

"Keep it," he repeated.

"Why on earth would you give me something so precious?" she asked, but was answered with silence. "Are you sure?" Charlotte frowned, knotting her brows together. "This isn't just something you give away on a whim."

"It looks good on you," he declared, ignoring her need to make logic out of the situation.

Charlotte eyed him curiously, but remained silent. Holding out her hand she admired the beautiful specs of turquoise that popped in the morning sun rays. "Thank you," she smiled at him, inadvertently missing the sign she had been inwardly dreading. *Welcome to Maryland.*

Chapter Ten

"Dimple, we have to go in eventually," Nicholas sighed, leaning his car seat back as far as it would go.

"I know. I know," she groaned. "Just give me a few more minutes."

"You said that a few minutes ago," he laughed. "I thought you were anxious to find out what was going on with your dad . . . you can't do that sitting in the car."

Closing her eyes, Charlotte inhaled deeply. *You can do this . . . just go in there and . . . and . . . and . . .*

"Dimple?"

Charlotte jumped. "Sorry. Let's just go to the hotel . . . I'll come back later."

"Later?"

"Yup. Let's go."

Nicholas watched her intently. "Are you sure?" he asked, bemused by her actions.

Charlotte let out a strained breath. "I can't go in there," she mumbled.

"Why not?"

"I haven't spoken to my family in a little over two years, and honestly, I had no intention of speaking to them anytime soon . . . ."

Nicholas nodded his head, patiently waiting for her to continue. In all honesty he had always wondered about Charlotte's estranged relationship with her family, but her reticent disposition gave him reason to pause whenever he thought to ask the back story behind their distance.

"Whatever . . . we're here now. Let's go in," she said decidedly, opening the door in one quick motion. The frigid Baltimore wind slammed into her, unremorsefully stinging her face with a vengeance. "We'll just stay long enough to find out what hospital my dad was taken to, and then we can leave."

Nicholas grabbed her trembling hand giving it a reassuring squeeze as they approached the long stoned sidewalk. Tilting her head back she met his gaze, a small smile touching her lips briefly, more for his benefit than hers.

"Knock," he urged her once they reached the large hunter green door.

Groaning in frustration Charlotte turned her face into his chest fighting the impulse to run back to the car. She thought that she could face her mother, but in truth she was still so angry, still so embarrassed. "I can't," she exhaled. "I've changed my mind . . . let's go back home. I'll call and check on him when we get back to the city."

Nicholas pulled Charlotte to him holding her quivering body against his. "You'll thank me later," he whispered into her hair before knocking on the door. The sounding thumps more forceful than what he had intended.

"No," she pleaded panic stricken. "Let go of me," she screeched under her breath.

"Charlotte!" Babet Toutant squealed throwing her arms around her daughter. "Manuel! Manuel! She's home!"

Manuel? "Daddy's here?" Charlotte asked, bewildered.

"And who is this?" Babet beamed, pulling Nicholas into a warm embrace. "Come in! Come in!"

"Hello, Ms. Toutant," Nicholas smiled at the middle aged woman. "I'm Nicholas."

"Please, please, call me Babet," she grinned, openly eyeing the man standing beside her daughter. "Charlotte isn't he quite the looker. You did good, sweetheart."

"Mom . . . I thought you said that dad was sick? He isn't in the hospital?"

"Hospital? Lord no. He's fine."

"But you left me a message saying that daddy was sick and that he needed to see me . . . I thought—"

"Well, I had to say something to get some fire under that stubborn hind of yours, otherwise, you would have never come back," Babet explained, her kind smile never faltering. "Nicholas, let me take your coat."

"Mom!" Charlotte yelled. "This is not okay."

"Charli Brown!" Manuel Toutant called as he turned the corner quickly making his way down the long narrow hallway.

"Daddy," she groaned, throwing her arms around her father's shoulders. "Mom's message . . . I thought . . . I thought . . . I didn't know what to think," she cried.

"I told that crazy old bat not to leave a worrisome message, but she was determined to do things her way," he said apologetically.

"And look! This 'old bat' got the results we all hoped for. Charli's home for Christmas." Babet clasped her hands together in quiet accomplishment. "This is the best present you could have given us," she pouted, pulling her daughter to her.

Charlotte heaved a sigh of frustration. "This isn't my present to you. You tricked me into coming here," she said through grated teeth while combing her fingers through her hair, seemingly irritated.

"Oh My Sweet Jesus! Manuel look at your daughter's hand," Babet shrieked, grabbing hold of Charlotte's hand admiring the sparkling diamond that sat comfortably on her ring finger. "You're engaged," she exclaimed, wiping at her moist eyes. "Manuel introduce yourself to your new son- in-law."

Manuel smiled warmly at Nicholas who had still been standing in the foyer. Extending his right hand he pulled the younger man into a gentleman's embrace, quick and informal. "I forgive you for neglecting the formalities," Manuel said, his voice low. "You can make it up to me later."

"Sir?" Nicholas frowned. "Formalities?"

"Mhmm. There's a certain decorum when asking a woman's hand in marriage, especially when that woman is my daughter."

"I didn't ask—"

"Baby don't be modest," Charlotte interrupted, withdrawing from her mother's arms and quickly making her way over to Nicholas who was staring at her quizzically. "Cat's out the bag now, right?" she giggled sweetly, her eyes pleading with him.

"Right," he said, arching an amused brow. "Cat's out the bag, indeed." Tightly wrapping his arms around her thin waist Nicholas pulled Charlotte into him, his full lips brushing against the hollow of her neck. "An explanation is going to be mandatory," he whispered before releasing her.

"What's done is done," Babet defended. "The important thing is that you're both here. Where are your bags? Manny help Nicholas bring in their things," she ordered, grabbing hold of her daughter's left hand once more. "Charli, I'm so happy for you. So happy. Wait until your sisters' see–"

"We're not staying," Charlotte explained, pulling away from her mother. "Daddy's fine . . . ."

"But–"

"I came because I thought something was wrong with my father, but he's fine– so I'm leaving."

"Well, that's understandable," Manuel said. "Still, you've been traveling for hours, and I'm sure Nicholas is hungry. Why not stay for dinner?"

"Daddy−"

"What's a few hours amongst family? What do you say Nick? Can I call you Nick?" Manuel asked the younger man.

"Yes, sir. Dinner sounds great," Nicholas agreed avoiding Charlotte's heated gaze. He could feel the anger radiating from her in deadly waves.

"I just bought a new pool table for my Man Cave. Come check it out . . . are you a Ravens fan? It's black and purple everywhere," the stout older man bragged pleased by his personal taste.

"Uh− I can't say that I am, sir," Nicholas frowned, laughter in his voice. "Giants fan all day. Blue and white runs through my veins."

"Born New Yorker?"

"Yes, sir."

"Then you're forgiven."

Charlotte stared after Nicholas as he followed behind her father, her expression was a bleak one. Their sole purpose of making the trip was to check on her ailing father. Beyond that she had no interest in being back in Baltimore— let alone of being around people who preferred to hurt her, rather than respect her feelings.

"Dinner," she said to her mother. "Dinner, and then we're leaving."

Chapter Eleven

The sound of laughter and dramatized merriment filled the dining room as the fifth round of English brew was passed around the dinner table. Charlotte looked on with blatant annoyance as her mother filled Nicholas' glass. "Don't you think you've had enough?" she asked snidely, rolling her eyes when he winked at her. He seemed to enjoy the art of riling her up, and was quite unashamed in his lack of concern over the matter.

"Oh Charli, let the man enjoy himself, won't you?" Babet intervened. "We're celebrating."

Charlotte sighed. "Any excuse will do I guess." Stealing a glance at her watch she smiled brightly at her parents forging sudden happiness. "Would you look at the time?" she gasped. "Hours feel like minutes when you're having a good time. I'll grab our coats."

"But it's so late," Babet complained. "Nick it's too late for you to make such a long drive back tonight."

Nicholas turned to face Charlotte with an uncertain look in his eyes. *Don't you even think about it*, she grimaced. Enough was enough and she would be leaving with or without him.

"Nick?" Babet whined, reaching across the table to touch his hand. "What's one night?"

"He drives long distances for sport, three hours is nothing to him, right Nicholas? A three hour drive is nothing to you?" Charlotte's expression held resolve, and it was apparent in the way she regarded him that she was at her breaking point. They had stayed long enough.

"Thank you for the offer," he began, "But—"

Babet looked from her daughter to the man sitting next to her and then back again. Narrowing her eyes at Nicholas she pressed, "Then if not for your own contentment . . . do it for mine."

Nicholas laughed uncomfortably. Looking at the older woman was like peeking at a glimpse of Charlotte in the future, their physical similarities were uncanny. "We don't want to impose," he said finally, looking to Charlotte for confirmation.

"I insist," she grinned. "How can you say *no* to your mother- in- law within the first few hours of meeting her? Shouldn't you be trying to win me over?"

Charlotte rose from the table placing her hand on Nicholas' shoulder as she did so. "Don't let her manipulate you . . . she's good at it."

Babet sighed outwardly. "Charlotte."

"Let's go," Charlotte said, dismissing her mother's feeble attempt at changing her mind.

"What's one night?" Manuel cut in. Rising from his seat he walked over to stand beside his daughter. "One night, and you can be on the road by noon tomorrow . . . what will it hurt?"

My mood, my pride, everything, Charlotte thought decidedly. "Daddy—"

"What do you say Nick?" Manuel smiled, bearing a full set of pearly whites.

"Uh. Sure, sir," he answered.

Manuel clasped Nicholas' shoulders. "Good man," he said before winking at his daughter. "What you have right here is a good man."

***

A bittersweet pain lingered in Charlotte's chest as she walked the stairs of her childhood. Passing old photos that lined the walls caused a sharp ache to linger in her chest. Long forgotten memories of her youth led the way to her once beloved bedroom. Charlotte froze when she reached the upstairs hallway, curiosity getting the better of her. Pulling her bottom lip into her mouth she took small steps toward the back room. Marguerite's room. Being there, in her parents' hallway, in front of her sister's bedroom felt surreal. Charlotte stopped just short of the doorway, closing her eyes briefly before turning the knob to the door she had years ago helped her younger sister decorate. Marguerite's room hadn't changed. Abstract art lined her walls from ceiling to floor amidst a bright sun kiss yellow gloss paint. The brightness highlighted large window panes and a white sponge blotted ceiling fan. The room in its entirety was chaotic, chaos at its best, yet while standing in the midst of it Charlotte couldn't help but smile whether it be from her failure to read between the lines all of those years ago, or from her ability to see through those lines now . . . she didn't know– still she smiled. Marguerite never played by the rules, confusion was her canvas, and disorder were the tools she used to create the madness all around her. *Is that what turned his head toward you . . . your lack of order . . . your ability to act on a whim with no regard for anyone else's feelings . . . your ability to create chaos . . .*

"Charli!" bellowed a familiar voice, "You're really here!"

Turning quickly to face her youngest sister, Charlotte gasped, "Adeline!"

"I can't believe you actually came home," Adeline laughed. "I thought I'd have to catch a mega bus to New York if I was ever going to see you again."

Charlotte's smile reached her eyes. Adeline had no filter, always saying whatever came to mind. "You're words are still as slippery as ever," she laughed. "What has happened in two years, Adie? You're taller than me . . . ."

"You've always been the short one," Adeline giggled. "That's nothing new."

Adeline resembled their father taking on his amber complexion and slanted hazel eyes, traits that skipped over both Charlotte and Marguerite. It was fair to say that of the three sisters, Adeline had inherited the more attractive features though she was too placid to take notice, or maybe it was her humbleness that made the apparent contrast unnoticeable, Charlotte never really knew.

"You cut your hair," Adeline smiled. "I like it," she said, combing her fingers through Charlotte's thick hair. "You look good, Charli."

Charlotte closed her eyes at the feel of her sister's gentle caress on her scalp, her small hands giving her comfort and a momentary peace— both were needed in abundance.

"I've met your fiancé," Adeline said, drawing Charlotte from her thoughts. "He's very attractive."

Oh. "Yeah, he is, isn't he?"

"Mom has him wrapped tightly around her finger . . . you should have warned him about her."

"I hadn't planned on staying long enough for her to get her claws into him," Charlotte admitted, shaking her head at her mother's foxlike ways. "That woman hasn't changed one bit," she laughed in spite of herself.

Adeline's laughter mirrored her sister's. "No, she hasn't . . . not at all. When are you leaving?"

"In the morning."

"Really?"

"Unfortunately."

Adeline laughed. "One night won't kill you . . . it's not like–"

"Did you know, Adie?" Charlotte choked out the words regretting them as soon as she had said them, but the question was already posed and she wasn't above making her younger sibling temporarily uncomfortable if it had meant finding out the truth. "About Marguerite and Todd, I mean . . . did you know?"

"No," Adeline answered without pause, her golden stare penetrative. "Do you believe me?"

Charlotte regarded her sister in silence for a moment as if in quiet deliberation with her thoughts. "Yes," she replied not sure if it was the truth.

Adeline smirked at her, her bright eyes alight with wry humor. "No, you don't," she said decidedly. Raising her hand to Charlotte's face she traced the outline of her brow. "Your eyes became hard just then," she smiled. "They tell on you every time . . . your eyes tell so many secrets."

"Is that so?" Charlotte smiled sadly.

"That's so."

"It's not that I don't believe you. I just—"

"It's just that everyone around you found it more convenient to lie to you rather than finding the courage to open their mouths to tell you the truth, and seeing how you were lied to by everyone else I understand why you wouldn't believe me . . . but I'm telling you the truth, I knew nothing about the two of them."

Charlotte nodded her head, satisfied by Adeline's words. It was an odd acknowledgement knowing that her seventeen year old sister had more common sense than the other members of her family.

"Have you and Marguerite spoken since . . . ."

"No," Charlotte answered, shaking her head forcefully.

"Oh. Do you think—"

"I have no thoughts in regards to her, none that are worth discussing at least." Charlotte's tone was curt as was her demeanor.

"Message received." Grabbing hold of her sister's hand Adeline led her out of Marguerite's bedroom and down the hall toward her own. "We have so much to catch up on Charli, tell me everything about your life in New York, and I mean everything," she giggled, raising a suggestive eyebrow at Charlotte.

A faint flush brightened Charlotte's cheeks. "Adie!" she squealed. "You're so . . . raw!"

"What? I'm curious," Adeline laughed.

"Well don't be . . . there are certain things between a man and woman that shouldn't be discussed in open conversation."

"What does that even mean?" the younger girl chuckled, an amused smirk on her lips.

"Privacy. Some things should be kept private, you know, not up for discussion."

"In our family everything is up for discussion . . . nothing is private," Adeline said as she pulled Charlotte into her room and closed the door behind them.

Swallowing her response, Charlotte meditated over Adeline's words in silence. Words of foolery and deceit. Her family had insisted on keeping hard truths private, and had left nothing up for discussion. She had been forced to live with the choices that others around her had made, and had yet to see the repercussions of their actions. Still, knowing all of this made no bit of difference and so contradicting her sister's understanding on their family's ethical values was a pill she'd rather not share.

"So are you going to tell me about New York, or not?" Adeline asked interrupting her thoughts.

Meeting her sister's gaze Charlotte forced a small smile. "New York is nice . . . life is good there . . . ."

"And?"

"And, I like it there."

Adeline shook her head discontented. "After two years of being away all you can say is that New York is nice, and that you like living there?" Smacking her lips she playfully pushed her sister's shoulder. "You have a fox down stairs with whom you happen to be living with in the liveliest city in the States, and you have no stories to tell?"

Charlotte nodded her head in silence.

"Interesting."

"What?"

"Engaged and in the Big Apple with no stories to tell . . . it seems unbelievable."

Charlotte's soft laughter filled the room. "You have no idea," she snickered, pulling at her hair with busy fingers. *No idea at all.*

Chapter Twelve

Charlotte walked into the kitchen and sat at the breakfast bar adjacent to the stainless steel sink. With her hands folded in front of her she stared blankly at her mother who had been braiding dough. The sight brought back memories of her childhood, of fresh baked holiday breads, warmed butter, and stovetop jams. Lost moments invaded her conscious reminding her of lightly burned fingertips and cartooned themed bandages. Memories of sitting in the kitchen for hours anxiously awaiting the opportunity to help her mother set the table, happy to be the eldest daughter− the daughter who earned the privilege of claiming the first slice of warmed bread. Thoughts of happier times filled her mind challenging her fury until she couldn't quite grasp the tightly wound rope that levitated her anger.

"Are you going to help me, or just sit there and watch?" Babet asked, intricately weaving her small fingers through the thick dough. Charlotte disregarded her mother's question with a side glance that spoke volumes. "Aren't you a few days short . . . since when do you bake braided bread before Christmas Eve?"

"That's usually how I go about it, but this year is different."

"How so?"

"Well, you're hell bent on leaving first thing in the morning . . . and Nick hasn't tried my bread yet, and the two of you won't be here on Christmas, so I thought it'd be nice to bake a loaf tonight."

"That's a nice gesture for someone you barely even know," Charlotte mused, her tone sarcastic.

"Knowing him well is of no consequence, he's your fiancé. Shouldn't that alone warrant kind gestures and such?"

If you say so . . . "Where is he, anyway?"

"Out back with your father piling salt in the paint buckets."

"Salt? Is it supposed to snow?"

"The forecast calls for a few flurries, nothing to trouble yourself over," Babet explained. Carefully knotting the layers of dough at each end she dipped her fingers into melted butter spreading the gloss evenly across the stacked twirls. Her hands worked quickly, confidently distributing their expertise without thought. "You should take Nicholas downtown. He mentioned that he's never been to the Inner Harbor."

"Oh."

"That would make for a nice date. I'm sure he would enjoy a night out in Baltimore before the two of you head back to New York."

"So now you're an expert on what Nicholas wants . . . you're baking him bread . . . making suggestions on his behalf . . . I guess the two of you hit it off pretty well for you to know so much about him in the short amount of time that he's been here," Charlotte retorted indignantly.

"Well excuse me for making a suggestion. My God, Charlotte what is wrong with you? You've been short with me since I've opened the door for you, and you're just as crass as can be . . . if I've done something to offend you, please, let me have it, and let's move on from it already, for peace sakes."

Charlotte sighed, awed by her mother's timely amnesia. *This woman cannot be serious right now? Has she done something to cross me? Really? Is omission not a committable offense? Seriously!* "Well if you have no recollection of slighting me— I must be the one with the problem," she offered, pushing against the counter space as she stood. "Good chat, mother, as always it was very informative."

"Charli—"

"And thanks for being so welcoming to Nicholas . . . I know how much *family* means to you."

"Charlotte—"

"Another time, mother, my fiancé wants to visit the harbor . . . after driving all of this way for nothing, it's the least I can do, right?" she smirked, her tone mocking. Turning slightly, she continued, "Thanks for the advice . . . you've always known best."

***

Bright lights and coral reefs decorated Downtown Baltimore illuminating the streets with seasonal merriment. Charlotte slowed her pace as Nicholas silently walked behind her taking in his surroundings. Night life in the city was at its peak as Christmas weekend drew closer. Couples walking hand in hand admiring colorful light displays in business owners' windows, shoppers lugging gift bags over their shoulders, tourist snapping photos of Baltimore's skyline . . . Nicholas took it all in.

"Damn, it's cold out here," he laughed, rubbing his hands together before bringing them to his face.

"You should have worn a heavier coat," Charlotte admonished. Turning around to face him, a bright smile softened her eyes. "You're shivering," she giggled. "Why didn't you wear gloves?"

"Gloves?" he frowned. "Have you ever seen me wear gloves?"

"You should always keep gloves in your pocket during the winter months, even if you don't intend on using them."

"What is that a lesson to the wise?"

"More to the fool . . . ." she laughed. "Here, put these on." Slipping her fingers from her pink leather gloves she handed them to him.

Nicholas raised a brow. "Seriously?" he laughed. "What am I supposed to do with these?"

"What do you think?"

"My hands are twice the size of yours . . . besides if I put them on what would you use?" he mused, handing them back to her.

Charlotte shrugged. "My hands are fine, it's yours I'm worried about . . . not everyone can handle a Baltimore winter," her words were teasing as was the smirk that played on her lips. He had been adamant in his belief that New York had the coldest winters around despite her explanation on what a Baltimore cold front felt like. The wind felt like jets of fire being shot at their insides as they drew closer to the harbor water.

"How much further do we have to walk?" he asked ignoring her banter.

"Depends on what you're in the mood for . . . what did you want to get into?"

Nicholas' bright grey eyes darkened at her words, his expression thoughtful. "You know what I like . . . surprise me." He spoke softly, but his voice was clear.

His words as always were playful and mischievous causing Charlotte to second guess the meaning behind them. His keen desire to get a rise out of her was beyond her understanding, and so she gave up trying to understand. Nodding her head North, Charlotte casually looped her arm through his. "Just over on Pratt Street there's this amazing Sushi restaurant, it's a local favorite . . . and the drinks are pretty cheap."

"Let's do it," he said ready to get out of the cold. Not that he would ever admit it aloud, but she was right- Baltimore's winter was nothing to play around with.

***

The restaurant was filled to capacity bringing the quaint establishment to life. People from all walks of life crowded the dining area shouting and laughing over spilled beer and empty glasses. Nicholas leaned into the table closing the space between the two of them. "So," he said, crossing his hands in front of him. "Are you going to give me an explanation?"

"An explanation?" Charlotte repeated, taking a sip from her wine glass.

"Let's cut the bullshit . . . you're lying to your parents about us being engaged . . . the undeniable tension in the room whenever you're around your parents . . . the reason your mother lied in order to get you here . . . pretty much all of it‒ are you going to give me an explanation?"

Charlotte eyed him from over her wine glass in deep contemplation. Considering the position she had forced upon him it was only right that she offered him an explanation, however, the thought of admitting the truth about her failed relationship with Todd seemed too much like confessing how pitiful her life had been before she had met him, before she had moved to New York, before she had started over. Knowing that Nicholas had viewed her on such a high pedestal gave her a sense of esteem that she hadn't felt in a long time.

Charlotte took a long sip from the glass before placing it on the table in front of her. Shrugging her thin shoulders under her loose fitting sweater she feigned indifference. "I had my reasons," she said frankly, meeting his gaze from across the table.

"I'm sure you did," he retorted. "I'm just waiting to hear them."

"You're patience has always been admirable."

"Charlotte, I'm serious." His tone lacked his usual laughter and charismatic charm. "No games . . . tell me what's going on?"

"I can't," she answered, looking away from him. There was no way she would be able to face him after divulging the most embarrassing part of her life. Wasn't living through the humiliation hard enough? Did she really have to speak on it as well? Her entire reasoning for leaving Maryland was to escape the mortification that had become her life—

that had become her very existence. Being alone in a strange city with only her thoughts to keep her company for months on end, with no family or friends to offer her solace when her mind worked against her, threatening to dishevel the very foundation of her understanding of the world and the worth of the people in it– was that too not enough? Did she really have to go into detail about such an unbearable time, a time that she still had not fully come to grips with, a time she still fought so hard to overcome? "I can't," she repeated, hating the words as soon as she had said them. "I'm sorry."

"You know everything about my life, literally everything, yet there is so much that I don't know about you," he sighed. "I don't know how to feel about that."

"I'm sorry."

"I don't want you to be sorry Dimple . . . I just want you to open up to me. Tell me something . . . anything . . . that would make this, make sense."

Charlotte looked down at her fingers avoiding his watchful gaze. Parting her lips to speak she quickly closed them groaning inwardly at her inability to open up to the one person who had proven his loyalty time and time again. "I–I just . . . I just needed . . . in that moment that's just who I needed you to be," she stammered hoping that her words would be enough for him.

Nicholas' molten gaze watched her intently. While part of him yearned for an answer beyond what she was willingly disclosing, the more sensible part hated seeing her fall apart over her inability to open up to him. Placing his hand on hers, Nicholas caressed his thumb along her knuckles. "Look at me," he demanded, his voice low.

Charlotte did as she was told, lifting her head to meet his gaze once more. The pain in her eyes was too much for him to bear. "Where to next?" he asked, pushing against the table as he stood.

"What?"

"I hope this wasn't your idea of showing me a good time? Where to next?"

"I don't–"

"We're going dancing," he said decidedly. Pulling Charlotte from her chair in one swift motion Nicholas smiled inwardly at the uncertainty in her eyes. "What?" he laughed. "What's up with that face, you don't like dancing?"

"I'm not the best dancer."

Nicholas shrugged, a wry grin flattering his soft features. "You're not the best communicator either, but we make due."

"Jerk," she laughed, her glum mood dwindling away rapidly. "And what, you're great at everything?"

"You haven't noticed?"

"Hardly."

Nicholas raised an eyebrow. "Maybe you should pay better attention."

"Maybe."

Taking Charlotte by the hand he pulled her toward the exit, his fingers tightly locked through hers. The feel of his strong hands on hers caused an immediate fluttering in her stomach, one that she couldn't quite explain.

"Where's the closest club near here?" he asked, interrupting her thoughts.

"The Latin Palace is walking distance from here."

"Latin Palace? Like Salsa dancing?"

"Amongst others . . . what are you an expert Latin dancer as well?" she snorted, looking up at him skeptically.

Nicholas met her brown gaze squarely. "I'm kinda' a big deal on any dance floor," he joked, amused by her annoyed tone.

"Oh? Well, then let's go."

"I'm just waiting for you to lead the way."

Chapter Thirteen

Nicholas scowled at the bright lighting pouring in through the wide bay window. Stretching his long torso, he pulled the thick chocolate comforter over his pale face, only then did he feel the hardness of the cold wooden floor beneath him. Turning onto his side, he glanced up at the high rise twin bed where Charlotte had been laying still fast asleep. The time of day was lost on him as was his ability to decipher reality from the pleasure state of lost dreams. Facets of the prior night's festivities played with his psyche, eluded remnants dangling just below the surface of his sub conscious. *So much for drinking the bare minimal,* he laughed to himself as the throbbing pressure of an unavoidable migraine worked its way into his frontal lobe.

"Knock. Knock. Are you guys awake?" Adeline whispered as she opened Charlotte's bedroom door. "Charli–"

Nicholas jumped up pulling the comforter with him as he did so, an act that he regretted immediately. The sudden movement jotted his senses, fueling the pain that was already making its way down his neck and into his shoulders.

"Sorry!" Adeline gasped, turning away from him. Covering her face with her small tan hands, she said, "I should have waited for you to tell me to come in. I didn't mean–"

"You're fine. I'm fully dressed," he assured her, letting the full comforter fall to the floor at his feet, revealing baggy grey sweat pants and a fitted black V- neck tee shirt. "Dimple's still asleep," he said, nodding in the direction of the bed.

"Dimple?"

Nicholas shrugged. "Charlotte."

Adeline smiled. "Dimple . . . that's different. I like it." Stepping further into the room she stole a quick glance at her sister before focusing her attention on Nicholas. Closing the distance between them, she gazed at him curiously. "You slept on the floor?" she asked, folding her arms across her chest.

Nicholas frowned under her inquisitive stare. "Uh, yeah, I did."

"Why?"

"Well, that's a great question . . . ." he exhaled, pulling his lower lip into his mouth as if in deep thought. ". . . a great question indeed."

"Were the two of you fighting?" she pressed, taking another step toward him, leaving no room between them.

Nicholas looked from her to Charlotte who still hadn't moved an inch. She looked so peaceful, so content . . . so beautiful. His steel grey eyes held her captive. It wasn't that he hadn't notice her apparent beauty. Beauty and Charlotte went hand in hand. But something was different, whether it be the quiet smirk at her lips, or the way her features were softened in her sleep, he didn't know. Knotting his brows together in silent deliberation he sighed before turning his attention back to the young girl in front of him.

"So?" she pressed, her frown deepening.

"So?"

"Were the two of you fighting?" she repeated.

"No."

"Then why were you sleeping on the floor?"

"You're a nosey little bugger, aren't you?" he grinned, hoping to evade her queries.

"And you're rather ambiguous," Adeline perked, perching her thin lips at him. Rolling her eyes into the air she shook her head at herself before exhaling dramatically. Tilting her head to the side, a small smile played at her lips. "I know this is going to sound insanely immature, and I would blame it on my age, but I'm sure it has nothing to do with the number of years I've been alive, or the lack of life I've experienced being seventeen and all. I just wanted to give you two the heads up that Marguerite and Todd are on their way here . . . I know it's silly, and that I'm probably an idiot for picking sides," she shrugged, "but I don't want Charli to have to go through the humiliation without even knowing that it's right around the corner . . . so if you two are indeed fighting– can you, for her sake deal with the problem later rather than sooner," Adeline groaned. "At least until you guys leave can you pretend to be the perfect couple for Charli's sake."

Nicholas took a step away from her, stealing another glance at Charlotte through his peripheral vision he narrowed his eyes, perplexed by Adeline's words. "Marguerite and Todd . . . who are they?" he asked, confusion evident in his tone.

Adeline's bright hazel eyes widened. "Charli never mentioned Marguerite to you?"

He raised an eyebrow, clearly in the dark. "Is she someone worth mentioning?" he replied.

Nodding slowly, Adeline stared at him stupidly. "I guess not."

"Adie," Nicholas spoke her name softly. "What's going on here?" he questioned.

"You should ask Charli–" she began before he quickly interrupted her.

"Charlotte likes to keep her secrets buried deep as I'm sure you already know. Marguerite and Todd, who are they?"

Adeline turned her head slightly, suddenly feeling awkward under his heated stare. It was as if he was looking straight through her, as if he was able to decipher her thoughts before she even spoke them. *Is he testing me, right now?* She wondered. "Do you really not know about Marguerite and Todd?" she asked, feeling uncertain.

Nicholas smiled at her sweetly. "If I did what reason would I have to pretend that I didn't?" he grinned, his handsome features coaxing her to divulge admissions that had little to do with her.

"Charli−"

"Will appreciate my knowing even if it comes from you," he assured her. Even though he knew that that probably wouldn't be the case in its entirety, he didn't care. In that moment, he wasn't concerned with any future misunderstandings, he would attest to them when the time came, however, as for now, he needed to know the truth.

"Marguerite is our sister. She's a few years younger than Charli . . . a few years older than me, and Todd is Charlotte's ex- fiancé− Marguerite's now husband," she sighed. Her words came out more like an announcement than an explanation.

Nicholas' expression bared his evident disgust. "What?" he grimaced.

"Charlotte walked in on them in her apartment a little over two years ago . . . they were . . . you know . . . and instead of fighting for Charlotte, he told her that he planned on marrying Marguerite, and that our parents knew about the affair," she said, her voice strained. "Charlotte emptied her savings and moved to New York a few weeks later, and hasn't been back home since— until now, and Marguerite and Todd are on their way here . . . ."

Nicholas gaped at her in silence not knowing what to say. What was a person supposed to say after hearing that? He didn't know. Groaning, he roughly combed his fingers through his thick disheveled hair. "It all makes sense, now," he laughed un-humorously to himself."

"What does?" Adeline frowned, glancing at her sister who still lay unmoving.

"Everything," Nicholas answered flatly. Squeezing her shoulders gently, he said, "Thanks for telling me."

"There's no need to thank me," she said decidedly, her tone even once more, the uncertainty in her eyes no longer evident. "A rain cloud for a storm?" she invited, her golden gaze hard.

Nicholas smiled at her sudden burst of confidence. "What does that mean?" he asked.

"A rain cloud for a storm . . . it's an old Creole saying. Why owe me later instead of paying your due now?"

"So in other words?"

"I told you what you wanted to know, now oblige me. Why were you sleeping on the floor? And why don't you know about the most heartbreaking moment in my sister's life? It doesn't quite add up?" she insisted, genuinely concerned.

Nicholas didn't respond. With a light shrug of his shoulders he smiled boyishly at her, his demeanor all of a sudden unforthcoming. It was his discreet manner that made her all the more curious, all the more intrigued.

"Fine," she glared at him, her eyes becoming tiny slits though she couldn't help but to feel amused. "You're quite the charmer . . . I hope you have my sister's best interest at heart."

"Your sister is very important to me," he offered, conveying nothing more.

Shaking her head, Adeline blew out a long breath. "I hope so," she smiled. "From the way she looks at you . . . it's clear that she loves you very much . . . I guess what I'm trying to say is, please don't hurt her. She's been hurt enough."

Nicholas' expression softened at her words, but a kind smile was all she received for them. He would play along for Charlotte's sake, especially now, knowing why she had wanted to save face about being in a relationship in front of her family, but he had no intention on outwardly lying to Adeline's face about his relationship with Charlotte, or lack thereof for that case. He couldn't in good conscience betray the young girl's trust in him, for whatever reason— he didn't know.

"Be good to her," she pressed, before turning away from him.

"Always," he whispered. "Always."

Chapter Fourteen

Manuel laughed under his breath as he skimmed through the comic portion of the morning paper. Raising his coffee mug to his thin lips he took a small sip from the China sampling the heat against his tongue before nodding his approval of the temperature. The smell of fried pineapples and chili seasoning filled the kitchen as Babet quickly worked her way around the large space emptying containers and coating pans with Coconut oil.

"Charli, stir the stew will you?" Babet asked as she opened the rice steamer. "Ashh," she cooed when moisture from the steam warmed her face. "Rapidement, avant qu'il ne brûle." *Quickly, before it burns.*

Charlotte sat stiffly on the bar stool adjacent to the breakfast bar. Regarding her mother intently she replied, "Depuis quand ne vous permettent cela? Je pensais que Babet était la seule femme qui pourrait toucher le ragoût?" *Since when do you allow this? I thought Babet was the only woman that could touch the stew?*

Babet laughed at her daughter's words. Shaking her head at her eldest child's insistent need to be combative she mumbled words under her breath, words that Charlotte couldn't quite catch. Babet blew on the rice before dropping her hand into the hot crock pot to scoop out a handful. "Try this," she ordered, still blowing on the rice as she made her way over to her husband. "Wet rice, just how you like it."

Manuel looked up from his paper long enough to taste the hot rice from his wife's hand. "Perfect," he complimented before taking another sip of his coffee.

"You see Charli, learn the taste buds of that man upstairs, learn them quickly, a man loves when his woman knows his desired taste for things. Comprendre?" *Understand?*

Charlotte slowly stirred the stew in silence. It amazed her how insensitive her mother could be. Did she not know that her advice was too little too late? Did she not care that every time she mentioned the do's and don'ts of a relationship her heart sank further into her chest? How could she not have known what she was doing? Wasn't maternal instinct a real concept?

Nicholas inhaled the unfamiliar smells as he descended from upstairs. Stopping just outside the kitchen he paused watching the interaction between Charlotte and her parents in silence.

Placing the wooden spoon back on the stove she turned to face her mother. "Why are you making so much food for just the three of you? Aren't you making dinner for the next two nights as well, that's a lot of food that'll go to waste?"

"There'll be more than just the three of us," Babet explained.

"Oh?"

Babet smiled broadly. "Turn on the news. Early this morning they announced that New York and New Jersey were going to get hit pretty hard with snow."

"The forecast says that all the time. It's generally not that bad," Charlotte snorted. "Regardless, whether it be snow, rain, or sleet I'm leaving as soon as Nicholas finishes getting ready."

"I doubt it," Manuel scoffed pointing at the small television that set just beyond the kitchen table. "I don't think you're going anywhere, anytime soon," he mused, raising his coffee mug in the air. "Salute."

Charlotte gawked at the television screen from afar striving to control her breathing as dread crept its way into her body leaving the feeling of trepidation in its wake. New York was covered in snow. It was like a nightmare that had come true. Staring at the small box in disbelief Charlotte listened as the charismatic news anchor bragged about the amount of snow that had fallen over night. "It's definitely going to be a white Christmas here in the Big Apple. Manhattan has been hit with two and a half feet of snow, and it's still early. The forecast clearly shows that this winter storm won't be letting up anytime soon. A possible State of Emergency is in effect. We will keep you updated as we find out more information, but until then folks stay off the roads, be safe, and stay warm," he smiled, waving goofily at his viewers.

Charlotte laughed though there was no humor in it. "Unbelievable. This is truly unbelievable." The thought of being stranded in Maryland for Christmas put a sour taste in her mouth. She prided herself on the fact that she had single handedly provided a place of solace away from the craziness that was the Toutant family, and yet when she yearned for it most it was inaccessible.

"Good morning, Mr. Toutant . . . Ms. Toutant. How is everyone doing this morning?" Nicholas asked, entering the kitchen with a wide smile on his face. "You look nice Dimple," he smirked, kissing her forehead before walking past her to sit at the table with her father.

"Please, call me Mom," Babet pressed, a blush rising to her cheeks. "You must be hungry. Charli throw a few pieces of bread in the oven, and make the man some eg—"

"Mom! Dad! We're here! Where is everybody? Whose Chrysler is that in front of the house?" exclaimed a loud squeaky voice from the foyer.

Charlotte's brows furrowed causing wrinkles to form around her narrowed eyes. She recognized that voice from the first words Marguerite had spoken. Turning to face her mother she opted not to hide the look of anguish that commanded her features. "How could you not tell me that she was coming?" Charlotte demanded, her hands trembling.

"It's the day before Christmas Eve, why wouldn't she come? She's family, she's your sister, your younger sister so be good to her," Babet replied, unfazed by her daughter's growing anger.

Charlotte let out a strained breath. "Be good to her? Am I hearing you correctly?"

"Mom?" Marguerite called from the hallway. The sound of muffled voices grew louder by the second.

"We're in the kitchen," Babet shouted.

Standing, Nicholas made his way over to Charlotte, pulling her tense body into the comfort of his arms. "Just breathe," he whispered into her ear stroking the back of her head with soft hands. "Just breathe."

"Mom, Todd's aunt baked you a carrot–" Marguerite stopped short at the sight of her sister. "Charli. I didn't know you were coming home."

Charlotte moved then, gently pushing against Nicholas' hard chest she turned to face her sister. Her gaze roamed from Marguerite to Todd who had been standing beside her, his arm wrapped through hers, his hand resting on her growing abdomen. *She's pregnant!* Her subconscious screamed at her mockingly. The moment she had desperately tried to avoid was transpiring, unraveling in front of her like a ribbon expended beyond its means, yet the rage she had expected to feel was non- existent. While the pain, and hurt of knowing what her sister had done to her was still very apparent, the anger dissipated.

"Charli, introduce Marguerite to your fiancé," Babet urged, drying her hands on her pants as she made her way over to her middle daughter.

"Babet, rester en dehors de celui-ci." *Babet, stay out of it,* Manuel muttered, not bothering to look away from his paper.

"Marguerite, your soeur is engaged! Charli introduce Nicholas to your sister and her husband," Babet cooed.

"No," Charlotte said flatly, amazed by her mother's nerve.

"Charli—"

Charlotte dismissed her mother's chidings with a wave of her hand, holding her sister's gaze she took her time walking past the two of them, quickening her pace only after being assured that she was no longer in their sight. Be it pride or immaturity she wasn't sure, nor did she care to justify or question her reasoning behind her actions. Making her way down the long hallway she allowed a brief smile to touch her lips. The man that she had hoped to spend the rest of her life with, the man who had brutally broken her heart had just been standing not five feet in front of her, and she could still breathe. Seeing him hadn't brought her to her knees like she assumed it would . . . she was still standing . . . she was still breathing.

Grabbing her coat from the wall rack she swung open the hunter green door allowing it to slam behind her. She needed to be anywhere but there. The frigid air worked as a healing agent numbing her body in all the right places.

"You feel like company?" Nicholas called from behind her, his smile sympathetic.

Charlotte stopped abruptly, allowing him to catch up to her. "Give me your keys," she demanded, averting eye contact. "I'll drive."

Chapter Fifteen

Placing her small hands on either side of the hot coffee mug that sat on the table in front of her, Charlotte closed her eyes as she inhaled the familiar aroma of Zeke's coffee shop. The smell of freshly brewed coffee and warmed desserts soothed her senses allowing her mind to sail away from the abyss that was intent on holding her captive. The depth of her hurt while not surface deep was no longer the grave entity that it had once been, and for that she was elated; still, to climb out of the suffocating void of despair without a ladder . . . a rope . . . or even a crutch, left her feeling baffled about the past thirteen months of torture she had inflicted on herself. *Was it all for nothing,* she wondered, as she stared into her mug, the blackness found there caused a frown to knot above her brow. "Do you know what's funny?" she asked, looking up to meet Nicholas' gaze for the first time since they had arrived. Not waiting for a response she continued, her big brown eyes fixed on his grey ones. "The bitterness of black coffee is insulting . . . the fresher it is the more bitter it tastes . . . most people steer clear of it," she laughed softly, looking down once more. "As humans we have this innate need to desire the sweeter things in life . . . overly processed truths that aren't real . . . that aren't good for us . . . not natural . . . but still we prefer it because of that engrained belief that sweeter is better . . . more enjoyable . . . more satisfying . . . all the while we are foolishly poisoning ourselves . . . ." Diverting her gaze, she turned her head away from him hating her inability to stop the moisture that fell shamelessly down her flushed cheeks. "Better to endure the bitterness of the unprocessed than the temporary satisfaction of forged sweetness," she whispered.

"Dimple-"

"I'm sorry," she smiled apologetically, forcing a quiet laugh for emphasis. "I brought you here . . .

into all of this madness. It's the holidays— you should be with your family enjoying yourself, but instead you're stuck here with me caught in a bogus lie. I'm sor—"

Nicholas moved then, reaching across the short round table he took her small hands into his large ones. "Look at me," he implored her, his voice barely above an octave. Shaking her head, Charlotte objected his command turning away from him to hide her humiliation. Allowing his hands to fall away from hers Nicholas lifted Charlotte's chin with gentle fingers forcing her to meet his molten gaze. Ignoring all inhibitions he slowly drew in closer to her closing the space between them. "There is nowhere else I would rather be than here with you," he said sincerely.

"You know about my sister and her husband?" she sighed. It was more of a statement than an actual question.

Nicholas furrowed his brows at her sudden forwardness over the matter. He hadn't thought that she would bring up the subject so boldly giving her knack for keeping things to herself. "Yes," he answered after a short pause.

Closing her eyes, she smiled sadly against his hand, fighting the urge to get up and run out of the crowded room. Her nightmares were coming to pass. "How do you know?" she asked, opening her eyes to look at him once more.

"That's not important."

"Did my mother tell you?"

"No."

"Don't lie to me."

Nicholas frowned at her allegation. "Dimple, have I ever lied to you?" he demanded.

"Then who told you?"

Dropping his hand from her face he groaned aloud. Telling her that Adeline had filled him in about their family drama would only cause more drama, and causing more problems within their family was the last thing he wanted to do. Nevertheless, his loyalty was to Charlotte not to her sister . . . not to her family. Weighing his options under her heated gaze made for an interesting change in his mood. Picking up his coffee mug for the first time since they had arrived, he took a sip of the cooled substance opting to remain silent.

"Nicholas?"

"Dimple," he sighed, wishing she'd drop the matter.

"My family . . . the people who I should be able to depend on the most have proven that they cannot be trusted, I've lost all trust in them. Are you going to hide things from me, too? Are you just as untrustworthy?" she asked harshly, her voice strained. There was something about the way she looked at him that made him feel uneasy. Her almond brown eyes glared heatedly at him until he felt forced to respond.

"Why does it matter who told me?"

"It was no one's place to tell you. If I wanted you to know I would have told you myself."

"One more thing I would never have heard," he snorted indignantly bringing the mug to his lips for another sip.

Charlotte huffed aloud. Leaning back in the wooden chair she asked, "What exactly is that supposed to mean?"

"You would have allowed me to stay clueless rather than being forthcoming about what took place between Marguerite and your ex."

"So what? Why does that have anything to do with you, or with our friendship? Do I have to tell you every part of my life?" she yelled. Nosey customers turned their heads in their direction, silently observing them from across the small café.

"No you don't *have* to tell me every facet of your life Charlotte, but it would be nice if you did. You know everything about me, everything about my adulterous mother, and alcoholic father. You know about my nannies who were better caregivers to me and my siblings than our own parents. You know about my failed relationships, and my sexual conquests, about my insecurities and asshole tendencies. You know everything about me, and I hoped that over time you would feel comfortable enough to let me in . . . comfortable enough to open up to me the way that

I have with you, but honestly, it feels like our relationship is a one sided thing and you don't trust me enough to—"

"To show my vulnerability?" she interrupted. ". . . to be weak around you."

"To be honest about your weaknesses!" Nicholas snapped, his tone harsher than what he'd intended. Sighing, he leaned back in the chair, closing his eyes briefly as he rubbed his fingers through his thick hair. Opening his eyes once more he met her gaze from across the table. "Look I'm sorry," he offered, his greys peering at her anxiously. "I didn't mean to raise my voice."

Charlotte gaped at him in silence fighting to keep her tears at bay. The anger she'd felt toward her family was being directed at the wrong person. Nicholas was undeserving to bear the brunt of her emotions, it wasn't fair to him. Pulling her bottom lip into her mouth Charlotte pouted at her predicament. Telling Nicholas the grotesque details about that surreal day seemed like a punishment for her heart, forcing her to relive that event again and again. *Fine,* she thought. *What's one more humiliating moment opposed to all the others?* "Todd and I met when we were ten years old. We were neighbors from the time we were in the fifth grade until his parents moved to York, Pennsylvania in the beginning of our senior year of high school. On weekends he drove to Baltimore to see me, and on holidays my parents allowed him to stay with us. Our families were really close. We applied to the same college in Virginia . . . graduated together, and then moved back to Maryland where we got an apartment that we lived in for four years. Best friends for fifteen years, dated for seven," she laughed sadly. "Engaged for two . . . it was a Saturday morning, and I got up early to run out to the grocery store . . . he had mentioned the night before that he had been craving chicken and dumplings and so I thought why not surprise him by making it before he had woken up . . . I ran to the store . . . my morning runs have always been important to me . . . you know that," she rambled, "I was gone for a little over an hour, and when I got back home I couldn't find my key so I knocked . . . I knocked hard, hard and loud, but he never came . . . I had to be in the hallway for a good couple of minutes before I became super irritated . . . I turned the knob out of frustration, and low and behold it wasn't locked. I clearly remembered locking the door, but being naïve and simple minded I paid that little detail no mind and proceeded into our home, put the groceries in the kitchen and stripped off my clothes . . . I was really sweaty, you know . . . I wanted to take a shower, and needed a towel so I walked into our bedroom . . . ."

"You don't have to say anymore—"

"I walked into our bedroom, and there they were . . . ."

"Dimple."

"Naked in the bed that we bought together. We slept on a blow up mattress for about four months before we were able to pay off our bedroom set," she smiled. Pausing for a moment she rubbed her index finger across her bottom lip. "We were just out of college, both working dead end jobs, but I was determined to make our home comfortable and so I worked over night at a loading factory for a little extra money . . . that was so long ago," she mumbled.

"Dimple, stop."

"All of that money saved all of those years ago for furniture that I wouldn't dare look at let alone sit on now," she giggled. The sound was labored, forced past her small lips. "My parents knew that they were sleeping together– they knew that he was engaged to the both of us at the same time, and that he was waiting for the right moment to end things with me. I was the fool blindly living a lie with no clue as to what was happening around me, and like wolves they all toyed with me . . . ."

"I'm sorry," he whispered, not knowing what else to say. What was he supposed to say to something like that? He was at a loss.

"You think that I opt to keep things from you because I'm not comfortable around you . . . because I don't trust you . . . you . . . you're the only person that I have in my life that I do trust. You're the only person who I can count on to be honest with me. But the idea of you thinking of me as a pathetic woman whose kid sister stole her fiancé killed me. My family knowing that it happened was bad enough . . . I just didn't want to be humiliated in front of you, too."

Her admission pulled at his heart. "Dimple, no one in their right mind would see you as being pathetic— especially not me. What took place between your sister and your ex was twisted."

"To say the least," she laughed softly. "Still, I felt the need to save face in front of you."

"Why?" he asked, a frown forming above his brow.

"I have my reasons," she whispered, pressing her lips together and sighing softly under her breath.

"Which are?"

"Mine," she giggled, meeting his gaze squarely. "Let's head back to my parents . . . I want to grab our things and go to a hotel."

Although his answering smile was empathetic, the look in his eyes seemed calculated, holding a resolve she had grown rather familiar with. "I appreciate what you're trying to do, but I'd rather you not get involved."

Nicholas' frown deepened. "I don't know what you're talking about."

"Yes, you do."

"Dimple," he sighed.

"It's a sweet gesture . . . you're trying to reconnect me with my family and all, but I'd much rather you leave well enough alone. I'm more than content with things being the way they are now."

Nicholas nodded his head as he processed her words, hearing the lies as soon as she had spoken them. "You only get one family, Dimple. Shunning the people who love you most in this world—"

"I have you . . . right?" she asked wide eyed.

Nicholas stopped short taken aback by her forwardness. Closing his mouth, he brazed his smooth knuckles along his rough jawline in silence. It wasn't her words that had given him reason to pause, rather the manner in which she had said them.

"Right?" she pressed, her big browns watching him intently, seeking an answer beyond that of which he was ready to divulge.

"Right."

"Then I' am content," Charlotte said hesitantly, her mouth becoming a thin line as she contemplated her thoughts, unsure on whether or not she should allow her intimate feelings to flow past her lips. Keeping the unspoken matters of her heart at bay seemed the logical thing to do— logic was never a lacking sentiment as far as she was concerned. "You're the only family I need."

Chapter Sixteen

Pulling up in front of her parents' home Charlotte paused before turning off the engine, fixing her gaze on Nicholas, she sighed dramatically. "I would love to be anywhere else right now."

"I know," he said, parting his lips slightly, his frown mirroring hers. "You don't have to—"

"We have nowhere else to go . . . hotels are booked up in this area and staying anywhere further away from the highway means more trouble if the storm hits Baltimore, too. As soon as they give word that New York is no longer under State of Emergency I want to be on the road speeding out of here."

Nicholas nodded. "Makes sense . . . so until then what do you want me to do?"

"What do you mean?"

"You told your family that I'm your fiancé."

"Yeah. And?"

"And before this morning we were under the impression that that lie would only have to last for a few hours yesterday, and this morning at the most . . . now we're stuck here until *further notice* . . . what am I supposed to make of that? I don't want to lie to your family for days on end . . . ."

"So you'd rather that I feel humiliated even more than I already am?" Charlotte mused, a knot forming between her brows. "You do know that I' am literally at my breaking point, right?"

"Dimple."

"Nicholas," she pressed, her dark brown eyes bearing into his hunted greys.

Sighing heavily, Nicholas rubbed his long fingers through his thick hair in deep contemplation for a moment, his expression exerting unspoken thoughts. Inhaling once more he licked his lips, his mouth agape though no words were spoken. There were so many things he wanted to say to her . . . so many feelings fighting to be heard, emotions that fearfully evaded the trespassing of his lips; yet unexpressed sentiments aside the needful look that haunted her gaze tore at his heart until there was only him, her, and the lie she had produced for the sake of her sanity.

"Okay," he said assuredly, reaching over to caress her chin with strong fingers. "But if we are going to make this believable we need to go all in. Actions speak louder than words."

"Actions?" she pondered. "Like what?"

"Well for one. We don't really embrace one another like an engaged couple would . . . you know, we interact like we're afraid to touch one another . . . always careful not to touch each other too much. It's hard to explain."

"Oh?" she whispered, averting her eyes. "Do we do that?"

"You haven't noticed?" he laughed softly.

"No," she lied. Charlotte shrugged nonchalantly seemingly un-phased by his observation of their habits. *Of course I've noticed,* she thought. *Whenever you touch me I get . . . .*

Shaking her head she aimed to silence the thoughts that had begun to creep their way into her subconscious . . . thoughts that she had fought long and hard to keep subdued— hidden even from herself.

"If we want it to be believable we have to interact like we're a couple . . . couples touch and embrace one another . . . are you willing to do that?" he asked.

"Of course," Charlotte grinned, though not certain if she whole heartedly meant it. Being in his arms would no doubt make things more complicated for her once they were back in the solace of New York, but that was a different battle for a later time.

Nicholas looked at her sideways, a slow smile forming at his full lips. "No holding back?" he smirked, testing her level of commitment.

"No holding back," she echoed, uncertainty concealed behind her practiced smile.

Chapter Seventeen

"Who wants to say *Grace*?" Babet breathed heavily, eyeing everyone at the table in one swift glance. When no one volunteered she focused her gaze on Charlotte who had been taking a long sip from her glass. "Charli?" Babet beamed, her eyes wide with anticipation. "Would you mind saying *Grace*?"

Charlotte glanced at her mother in dismay. Of all times to be put on the spot it had to be at a moment when she vowed absolute silence. Smiling through her annoyance, she closed her eyes and breathed inwardly, silently asking The Lord to give her the words to speak. *"Father we come to you in humbleness asking that you bless this food that we are about to consume for the nourishment of our bodies. Keep us in your mercy and continue to cover us by your*

blood because we know that if it were not for you we would have nothing, and that this meal would not be before us. Allow us to govern ourselves according to your will, and give us all peace that passes all understanding. In Jesus name we pray, Amen."
Opening her eyes she stared down at her plate, a blank expression on her face.

Babet reached for the mashed potatoes as she simultaneously pulled her dinner plate closer toward her. "That was beautiful honey," she smiled brightly.

"It really was," Marguerite agreed, a weary smile on her lips.

Charlotte looked up from her empty plate to meet her sister's gaze for the first time since they sat down for dinner. It amazed her how she could even open her mouth to utter a word let alone a phrase to her. Marguerite batted her charcoal eyes in attempted innocence but the act was as unacknowledged as it was uninvited. Her coyness was as worthless as her failed attempt at making amends.

"Nicholas," Adeline said, dramatically clearing her throat, unintentionally drawing everyone's attention to her. "Tell us about how you proposed. I bet it was really romantic?"

Nicholas smiled broadly at her before turning his attention to Charlotte who had been sitting quietly beside him. "I don't know if I'd call it romantic."

"Tell us!" she gushed. "Did you get down on one knee? Did she cry?"

Nicholas narrowed his eyes at Adeline, a boyish smirk teasing his lips, catching her attention and causing her to quickly divert her hazels from his greys. His charm was unnerving and she was sure that he knew it better than anyone.

"She must have been giddy?" Adeline continued, her eyes focused on the napkin resting to the left of her plate hoping that in looking away from him, she would gather her thoughts more vigorously.

Nicholas laughed softly at the young girl sitting across from him hoping that no one else caught their little standoff. He couldn't help but tease the girl, her nosiness proved unsettling. Still, she had already brought up the topic of interest and as he expected all eyes were on him awaiting his response to her train wreck of questions. "Charlotte was—"

"I was beyond shocked when he proposed," Charlotte interrupted, a huge smile brightening her complexion. "We were lying in bed, it was Christmas morning of last year . . . I remember it being so cold outside . . . New York winters are nothing to play with— yet I was so warm in his arms. I didn't want to get up let alone move, but he insisted that we get out of bed," she giggled, turning to face Nicholas who was watching her closely. "I should have known that he was up to something, he was so adamant about opening presents. We took turns opening our gifts laughing at the fact that we both bought each other mostly the same things . . . tunics and perfume for me and cardigans and cologne for him. It's amazing how much we think alike." Tilting her head to the side Charlotte traced the outline of Nicholas' 5 o' clock shadow, holding his gaze captive as she did so.

"Just when I thought we were finished, and I had begun to clean up he told me that I hadn't opened all of my presents," she sighed, the sound was one of fulfillment. Turning her attention back to Adeline who like the rest of her family was engulfed in her story, Charlotte smiled brightly. "Looking around the tree I couldn't see anything left for me to open so I turned to face him . . . that's when my heart dropped . . . he was down on one knee with this ring in the palm of his hand," she cried, holding up her left hand with the blue topaz diamond sparkling for all to see. "He told me that he had never loved another person as much as he had loved me, and asked me to spend the rest of my life waking up to him so that he could show me just how much loving me meant to him, every day, for the rest of his life."

"Oh my Lord! That is perfection if I ever heard of such a thing," Babet gushed.

"Something out of the movies," Adeline agreed, wiping her eyes with the back of her hands. "I'm so happy for the both of you. It's so amazing that you went to New York and met such a sweet guy."

"Amazing that she went to New York and met him?" Manuel scoffed. "No offense Nicholas, but you do know that you're the lucky one, don't you? Charlotte is as good as it gets."

Nicholas smiled kindly at the older man, "I know that well, sir."

"The two of you haven't known each other that long. Why rush marriage?" Todd asked. Though his tone was impassive it wasn't hard for Nicholas to see the hidden emotion right beneath the surface of his words.

Nicholas shrugged his shoulders nonchalantly. "I wouldn't say we're rushing into anything. If a man wants something he should do whatever he can to acquire it."

"I just think two years isn't an adequate amount of time to truly get to know someone. After years—"

Charlotte laughed sardonically. "After years and years someone can still be a stranger to you, or was that not a concept you taught me best?"

"Charlotte—" Marguerite began.

"And please . . . Don't get me started with you."

"All I'm trying to say is that rushing into a marriage never made anyone happy," Todd continued despite Marguerite's stiff hand on his leg urging him to remain silent. "I'm sure this man makes you happy in his own way, but to force marriage—"

"Excuse me?" Charlotte shouted. "Who do you think you are to question the validity of anything, let alone my engagement?"

"Dimple, calm down," Nicholas whispered into her ear, his large hand caressing her cheek as his thumb prompted for her to look at him. "Everyone has the right to their opinion, even if it isn't warranted, right?"

"Still—"

Leaning into her, Nicholas gently pulled Charlotte to him closing the small distance between them, his fingers lightly wrapped at the base of her neck. Parting her lips to speak Charlotte offered nothing to the silence of the room, words were lacking as was her ability to process what was about to happen. Like the fair hairs of a dandelion his lips tinted hers, teasing her senses until her flesh tingled from the excitement of his closeness. Soft petals of blown daisies floating from the coolness of a breeze, his mouth caressed hers until she was opening for him, allowing his soft tongue entry into the warmth of her mouth. Time stopped along with her heart as she melted into his embrace, blind to the knowledge of where one began and the other ended— in that lapse of time they were one and the awareness that her family had been watching their embrace was circumstantial to the unknown feelings that were quickly making their presence known. His mouthed caressed hers, hypnotizing her senses and overtaking a part of her that had never been awaken. Taking his time, Nicholas slowly pulled away from her ending their kiss with a tug of her bottom lip, the small bite adding a pleasure pain sensation there.

    Nicholas regarded her carefully, his molten grey eyes holding her captive. Blinking rapidly,

Charlotte swallowed hard as she raised a trembling hand to her sensitive lips. Her reaction made him smile. Turning his attention back to the plate of food in front of him, Nicholas avoided making eye contact with the others around him afraid that his amusement over their ordeal would get the better of him, and the last thing he wanted to do was laugh in Todd's face even if the man deserved it.

"If you would all excuse me . . . I need some fresh air," Todd announced, abruptly rising from the table not waiting for a response before he briskly walked out of the dining room and down the long hallway toward the front door.

Feeling that all eyes were on her, Marguerite kept her gaze fixed on the table unable to meet the stares of her family. "Please excuse me," she said softly, a forlorn look on her face as she backed away from the table and went after her husband.

"Aye, Papa peut vous me passer le macaroni, s'il vous plait?" *Aye, dad can you pass me the macaroni, please?* Adeline asked, un-phased by her brother- in- law's behavior.

Manuel shook his head in protest. "Vous mangez trop. Vous obtenez la graisse." *You eat too much. You're getting fat.*

"Ay - ya- ya- ya," Babet moaned. "Vous ne pouvez pas dire une adolescente elle devient la graisse, il va ruiner sa confiance," *You can't tell a teenage girl that she's getting fat, it will ruin her confidence.*

"Elle est la mère Bon je ne suis pas manque de confiance me passer les balles de citrouille." *It's okay mother I'm not lacking in confidence pass me the pumpkin balls.*

Charlotte giggled aloud unable to keep her laughter at bay at the exchange between her parents and her baby sister. Adeline had grown into such a beautiful, self- assured young woman who had learned early on how to hold her own against their over assertive parents. Ignoring her father's words she passed the bowl of cinnamon drizzled pumpkin balls to the bright eyed younger girl. "Elle est une fille de plus en plus. Voici Adeline, manger plus, plus, plus," *She's a growing girl. Here Adeline, eat more, more, more.*

Babet shared in her oldest daughter's laughter taking the bowl of macaroni from her husband's hands and piling it on Adeline's plate. "Manger plus, plus, plus." *Eat more, more, more.*

Nicholas smiled at Charlotte who for the first time since they arrived seemed to be at ease with being around her family, and the thought made him happy.

"Nick, I feel sorry for you . . . marrying into this family of troublesome women . . . poor man with bad luck," Manuel groaned.

"A few minutes ago you told him that I was a catch," Charlotte smiled. "You changed your mind rather fast."

"You're no good just like your mother. Troublesome woman," he grumbled as he rose from the table.

"I love you, too, papa," Charlotte chuckled, ignoring her father's words.

It had been over two years since she had laughed with her family, since she had broken bread with them, since she had spoken French. Stealing a quick glance at Nicholas she felt thankful to him for pushing that they stay. The relentless feeling of anxiety had been a never-ending cloud on her spirit from the time they had left Manhattan. The persistent yearning to escape the house she had grown up in had clung to her like a second skin, always there— always present . . . to get in the car and head back to New York with no desire of ever looking back was a need beyond what words could describe, however, in those few short lived moments of laughing with her parents and seeing Adeline's golden eyes light up with amusement, Charlotte couldn't help but feel a sense of home. The familiarities of tradition and what it meant to be surrounded by her family. In those few seconds she had all but forgotten the damage that her loved ones had inflicted on her— the feelings of pain and betrayal were non-existent in that moment.

"You two must be exhausted," Babet sighed, interrupting her from her thoughts. "Go upstairs and get ready for bed."

"Dinner was delicious, thank you," Nicholas smiled.

Babet waved her hand in dismay. "No thanks necessary. You're my son now. What is thank you among family?"

"Good night, mom," Charlotte said, returning her mother's smile. "Merci." *Thank you.*

Chapter Eighteen

Standing in the middle of her bedroom Charlotte waited until Nicholas closed the door before she exhaled a sigh of relief. They had gotten away with their first onset of group interrogations and she couldn't have been more relieved. Throwing herself onto her mattress, she pulled off her shoes and socks quickly wrapping her slender body in the duvet that lay across the bottom of her bed. Her mother was right about one thing, she was exhausted, beyond exhausted. The thought of being found out was mentally draining. *Thank God for Nicholas!* She thought, rolling to her right so that she was once again facing the center of her room. Nicholas sat at Charlotte's desk quietly watching her every move.

"So what was that kiss about?" she asked after a moments time breaking the silence between them.

"It's called acting . . . you know, what you asked me to do."

"I never *asked* you to kiss me."

"The moment called for it, and so I took one for the team. You're welcome," he smirked boyishly at her.

Rolling her eyes she reached for one of the many throw pillows that rested against her footboard and flung it in his direction. "I'm welcome? You're so full of yourself."

"Yeah, you're welcome. What you experienced was an Academy Awards performance. Do you know how much actors get paid for the job I'm working for free, be appreciative," Nicholas smiled, his silver eyes alight with mischief. "What about you and that engagement story? You're better at telling stories than you are at editing magazine articles, maybe you should consider switching to the writing team," he joked. Leaning back in the black cushioned chair he rested his hands behind his head.

"And you're a way better actor than you are Editor-in-Chief, perhaps you should use a portion of your trust fund money to jumpstart a career in Hollywood."

"Whether it be Editor-in-Chief in New York, or on the scene in Hollywood I'm sure I'd be equally successful. I pride myself in being great at all of my endeavors."

"Is that so?" Charlotte laughed.

"You didn't know? You witnessed it for yourself downstairs."

"Wait. Is this your lame attempt at asking if you're a good kisser?" Charlotte snorted.

"That would be a rhetorical question . . . of course I'm a good kisser."

"Don't be so arrogant."

Nicholas raised an eye brow. "Stating a fact isn't being arrogant."

"Shouldn't I be the one calling facts, facts, since I am the one who was kissed by you? I should be the judge on whether or not you're a good kisser."

"Your body language answered any questions I may have had about your thoughts on my kissing ability."

Sitting up Charlotte crossed her legs under her. Tucking her wild hair behind her ears she licked her lips in deep thought. "What do you mean by that?"

"Your body answered any questions I may have had."

"I heard what you said . . . I don't understand what my body language had to do with anything."

"Your hands were shaking under the table."

"They were not," she exhaled, exasperated by his cockiness.

"Well they weren't lying idly on your lap. Don't be embarrassed I've been known to have that effect on women."

Charlotte laughed suddenly, the sound loud in the small room. "I–" she paused, her brows knotted together at the sound of hard knocking on her door. "Who is it?"

"Can I come in?" asked the familiar voice.

Todd. Charlotte looked to Nicholas who was seemingly uninterested in their visitor.

"Come in," Nicholas answered, his cool gaze still on her.

Todd opened the door, but remained standing in the hallway. He looked agitated, his face a twisted mask that held resolve. "I thought we could go outside for a beer," he shrugged, resting his shoulder against the door frame.

Nicholas eyed the other man curiously, "Sure," he said after a second's delay. "You good with that, babe?" he asked Charlotte, a small smile toying with his full lips.

"Don't be too long," she cooed, stretching her long torso across the bed. "I can't go to sleep without you."

Rising from the chair he gestured for the shorter man to lead the way, winking at Charlotte before leaving the room.

Pulling the duvet over her body once more she wondered what Todd could possibly have to say to Nicholas, but her mind drew a blank. The idea of them sitting on the front porch conversing made her brain hurt. Todd was indeed a vile excuse for a human being, but Nicholas was more than capable of handling his own affairs when it came to the other man. Closing her eyes, Charlotte snuggled under the thick cover, settling into the peaceful mood that Nicholas had left behind. For the first time in so long she felt content.

***

"Congratulations," Todd said, handing Nicholas a cold beer before sitting on the wooden porch fence. "Charli is a good woman . . . she deserves to be happy."

"I concur," Nicholas agreed taking a small sip from the dark glass bottle.

Looking out into the empty yard Todd asked, "Has she told you about us?"

"I know bits and pieces."

"I know from the outside looking in it's easy to place judgment, but in my defense I went seven years with no sex . . . not too many men would be able to last that long and still be faithful . . . I'm not making an excuse for what happened, but to live with a woman who was dead-set on staying a virgin until marriage, but then when asked to set a date she only made excuses . . . what was I supposed to do?" Todd rambled more to himself than to Nicholas who was watching him closely.

"Not sleep with her sister," Nicholas offered, sarcasm strong in his tone. "Anyway, why are you telling me all of this? It's a little weird don't you think . . . my fiancé's ex fiancé explaining to me why he cheated on her with her sister . . . ."

"Is she making you wait?" Todd asked suddenly.

"Are you serious?" Nicholas laughed. "You asked me out here to inquire about your wife's sister's sex life?"

Todd glanced at Nicholas inquiringly with no desire to withdraw his question from their conversation. "Is she?" he demanded, his expression hardening.

Frowning, Nicholas narrowed his eyes at the man before taking another sip from his beer. "What is or isn't happening in between my woman's legs is none of your damn business," he said matter- of-factly. "Let's not cross any lines that can't be uncrossed."

"She was with me for—"

"And now she's with me, and you're with her sister . . . like I said let's not cross any lines that can't be uncrossed. Thanks for the beer."

Chapter Nineteen

The light sound of breathing stroked her senses until she was pulled completely from the world of unconsciousness. Blinking rapidly in the darkness, Charlotte repositioned her body under the thick white comforter settling her smaller frame in the warmth of Nicholas' as her eyes worked to adjust to the dark room. Closing her eyes once more she listened as he inhaled and exhaled, finding peace in every breath he took. Turning over, Charlotte stared at the man beside her. Hesitantly, she ran her thumb along his jawline, smiling at the sensations the prickly hair there had left behind. Hues of cinnamon and bronze shaded his goatee blending together with such brilliance—he was beautiful. Leaning into him, Charlotte traced the outline of his thick eyebrows following the path from his button nose to his high cheekbones stopping just short of his lips. Inhaling silently, she moved closer still, closing her eyes once more as she allowed her lips to touch his, once, twice. Sighing, Charlotte slowly moved away from him, glancing at the alarm clock as she climbed out of bed. *4:17a.m.*

Quietly she tiptoed down the short hallway that led to the narrow wooden steps hoping to not wake anyone along the way. She needed some fresh air to gather her thoughts. Too much was happening and she wasn't quite sure what to make of it. The anger she had whole- heartedly felt for her parents was dissipating though she wasn't quite ready to forgive them, and unrequited feelings for her best friend were starting to plague her thoughts despite the fact that she had worked so hard to keep those feelings at bay. *It's this house!* She thought. *That's all it is . . . it's being back at this house with all the madness, and all of my family buzzing around me . . . they're confusing me . . . being here is confusing me.* Avoiding the areas of the floor that she knew would creak with even the lightest of touches Charlotte inched across the living room making her way to the kitchen. The light was on. Quickly stopping in her tracks she peeked around the long white wall that separated the two rooms. *What is he doing up so early?* She wondered, staring at the back of her father's head. *Ugh! There are so many people in this house . . . so much for clearing my mind.*

"Are you going to stand there staring at the back of my head, or are you going to come in and have a seat?" Manuel asked without turning around.

Charlotte jumped. "How did you know I was behind you?"

"I didn't serve twenty years in the military, survive wars, and put up with your mother for all of these years to not know when I'm being spied on. I could feel your eyes on the back of my neck," he smiled.

"What does mom have to do with any of it?" Charlotte mused aloud.

Manuel laughed. "Your mother is more dangerous than any war I've experienced."

"And more worrisome, too, I imagine."

"Oh, well, her heart is in the right place. It doesn't do any good to be so hard on her," Manuel defended his wife as he gestured for his daughter to sit in the empty seat across from him. "Why are you up so early?" he asked.

"I could ask you the same thing," she shrugged, ignoring his reprimanding words.

A slight grin touched Manuel's small lips as he raised his navy blue coffee mug in the air before bringing it to his mouth for a taste of the lukewarm bitter substance that tinted the inside. "It's nothing like fresh coffee before sunrise."

"Would you mind pouring me a cup?" she asked, grabbing a mug from the sink strainer before taking a seat across from him.

"Of all the things I do mind, that isn't one of them," Manuel laughed. "So . . . ."

"So . . . ."

"You're engaged . . . ."

"So it would seem."

"Are you happy?"

"What's happy?" she asked, gliding her pinky finger along the edge of the cup.

Manuel frowned. Deep lines etched above his brow showing his age through his weary expression. "What's happy?" he repeated, narrowing his golden eyes at his oldest daughter.

"I'm asking, what's happy? What does it mean to be happy?" Raising the hot cup to her lips Charlotte took a small sip as she gazed at her father over the brim of her mug, her wide eyes gazing quizzically into his.

"Charlotte you've had many happy moments over the years. I'm sure that you know what it means to be happy."

"Do I?" she laughed sadly. "I don't believe that I do. I know what contentment feels like. I know what achievement feels like. I know what joy feels like, but happiness? I don't know if I honestly know what that emotion feels like," she shrugged. "Do you? Do you know what it feels like to be happy?"

Manuel sighed. "If Nicholas doesn't make you happy, why in the world did you agree to marry him?"

"This isn't about Nicholas. This is about me, Charlotte, asking her father if he knows what it feels like to be happy."

"Yes, I know what happiness feels like. Every morning that I wake up to your mother, I am happy. Every night that I close my eyes knowing that my children were safe throughout the day, I am happy. Knowing that God's grace and mercy has kept me even when I didn't deserve it, I am happy. It's the little things that make me happy. The things that may not feel like much to other people means the world to me. Like seeing you walk through that front door the other day that brought me much happiness."

Placing her mug back on the breakfast bar Charlotte asked, "Why?"

"Why?" he repeated. "Because I love you . . . I love all of you."

"Love is a wasted emotion."

Manuel laughed then- the sound lightening the sullen mood instantly. "You don't mean that," he smiled.

"I don't?" Charlotte challenged, raising an arched brow at her father.

"I'm not blind. I see the way you steal glances at Nick. Your eyes light up whenever he is close to you. And the way he looks at you . . . for two people who have promised themselves to one another you have a strange way of showing affection, it's awkward, and hard to explain, but there is much love there."

Charlotte remained silent. Taking another sip of her coffee she fought back the tears that were threatening to fall from her eyes.

"There's much love there, and much happiness," he continued.

Silence.

"Todd cheated on your sister, and got the other woman pregnant. Marguerite is due a few weeks before his mistress."

Charlotte gasped. "What?" she demanded, surprised by her father's words.

"Some woman he works with . . . apparently the affair was going on for some time. Your sister asked him to resign and find employment elsewhere— insecure of the fact that he worked so closely to the woman he was sleeping around with, but he refused."

"What?" she repeated, completely shocked.

"So you see my dear you giving up on love, and walking around with a chip on your shoulder doesn't make things better for you, nor does it change the fact that the person you hoped to end up with just wasn't the one God had picked for you. We think we know what's good for us, but we later find out that we were wrong all along . . . we don't know much about anything."

"Marguerite must be devastated."

Manuel yawned as he rose from the wooden stool. "The weather broke in New York early this morning. All things eventually come to an end. That's just the way nature intended. It was nice seeing you, Charli."

"You too, dad," she whispered.

Chapter Twenty

Unlocking her apartment door Charlotte let out a sigh of relief. She was *home*. Finally out of the lion's den, and she couldn't have felt more relieved. Quickly making her way through the small foyer she pulled off her boots as she walked down the narrow hallway that led to her kitchen. "Do you want something to drink?" she asked Nicholas who had been carrying her luggage into the living room.

"I'm fine," he answered. "I didn't want to say anything on the road because I know how anxious you were to leave, but now that you're home do you think that maybe you should call your parents and tell them that we left?"

"I'm sure they figured it out by now."

"Still, it's your parents . . . at least send them a text message."

"I left a note near the coffee pot. I'm sure they've already seen it and they're fine. Right now my mom is probably smashing yeast onto a floured counter space, and annoying my dad with her Christmas classics which are more than likely playing in the same rotation," she giggled.

"Call them," Nicholas insisted. Unhooking Charlotte's purse from her suitcase he carried it into the kitchen and handed it to her with a look of resolve in his eyes. "It's Christmas Eve."

Charlotte sighed. "Fine," she breathed indignantly. Snatching her purse from his loose grip she opened the large bag in search of her phone. Frowning, she glanced up at Nicholas before pulling out an envelope with her name written across the front. "Do you know anything about this?" she asked, holding the envelope up in front of him.

Shaking his head, Nicholas denied the charge. "Open it," he urged, leaning against the kitchen door frame and resting his weight along the wooden panel.

Charlotte,

If you're reading this it means that you've gone back home- if I should even call that place your home. Maybe for the mere sake of wanting to get away from me, from your family, you have convinced yourself that New York is the place for you . . . honestly I don't know. I can't say that I know much about anything these days.

I'm writing this letter to apologize for worrying you- as you know by now your father isn't sick. I shouldn't have lied, but in the past two years I have called you and left message after message just for you to ignore me as if I never had the title of being called your mother. And so, I told a little white lie to get you to come home for the holidays. If you knew how much I've missed you, how much your father and sisters have missed you . . . I'm sure your heart would be sore just as ours has been these last couple of years.

Charlotte last year I was diagnosed with Multiple sclerosis. Apparently, I've had it for some time . . . I wanted to tell you face to face, but I couldn't. There seemed to be other pressing matters on your mind, and I didn't want to be a burden. I know you partially blame *your father and I for what happened with Marguerite and Todd. The fact that we knew about the affair, yet let you continue on with him as if nothing was going on behind your back seems like the worst thing parents could have done to their child, to their daughter, but Charlotte, my beautiful most precious one- you have to understand the position we were placed in. Devastation and destruction were the inevitable in such a situation, but that wasn't what kept us from telling you such a despicable truth, it's not why we hoped such a hideous secret would stay in the dark. The thought of losing you . . . I couldn't imagine . . . the thought of not being able to see you every day broke my heart more than you could ever possibly fathom. And I knew that if you had found out about the affair . . . that if you knew the truth- it would only be a matter of time before you left me. You would leave me; you would leave your mother who knows you better than anyone else on this earth all for the means of wanting to escape. And what a selfish woman I am that I didn't want you to go. I would have rather that you lived a lie if it meant that I would get to have you close to me. I'm a monstrous woman. A self-serving woman. A terrible woman. But I am a woman who loves you more than I love any other creature that has ever been blessed to walk God's Earth, and for you I believe that is a blessing and a curse. Charlotte, of all my loved ones- you are my most beloved and I couldn't stand to be without you. Of all I have done to keep you with me . . . in doing so I have pushed you further away. I am sorry. Those three words are echoed in my brain every day I open my eyes, and every night before I close them. Forgive us.*

One day you'll understand the angst of having a child that you love even more than the truth.

Mom

Charlotte closed her eyes fighting to hold back the tears that were seconds away from spilling past her already swollen lids. Exhaling, she silently folded the letter and put it back into the envelope, hoping that the pain she felt wasn't deeply etched in her expression.

"Who's it from?" Nicholas asked after a moment.

"My mom."

"Is everything okay?"

"Yeah, it's fine. I could use some air . . . let's go out for a drink or something?" she said inching past him. Her apartment suddenly felt too small . . . too constricted. She needed to be outside where the bitterness of the winter air would aid in numbing her thoughts. "Are you coming?" Charlotte asked when Nicholas didn't move.

"When are you going to stop running?" he answered her, ignoring her impatient demeanor.

"What? Running? Who's running?" Charlotte mumbled as she hurriedly pulled at the collar of her coat. Her level of frustration was quickly rising as was her need to be out in the open.

Nicholas stared at her shrewdly. "It seems to be your answer to everything. Whenever things don't go as planned, or when you feel that you aren't in control your answer is to run away. Charlotte turning away from your problems isn't going to help anything. You have to learn how to face your demons head on."

"My demons? I don't think my demons are the ones that are haunting me. It's everyone else–"

"Stop running."

"This isn't about me running!" she snapped at him. In that moment anger was a living entity slowly crawling up her body and settling at the tip of her tongue. "Why in the hell do you even care so much anyway? You've done your due- diligence as my friend, and I am so thankful but you can leave now."

"Stop running," he repeated, unstirred by her agitated disposition.

"Nicholas, I am so serious right now, leave."

"I'm not going anywhere and neither are you. We don't have to talk about the letter. That can totally be a closed case if it's not something you want to talk about, but I'm not leaving you here to wallow in self- pity, and I'm not going to let you wander the streets feeling sorry for yourself."

"What do you want me to do?" she screamed. "You have all of the answers, right? You know everything about everything so tell me . . . what is it that you want me to do?"

Nicholas tilted his head to the side, narrowing his greys at her. "Get over it," he advised simply.

Charlotte laughed as she swiped at the onslaught of unwanted tears that carelessly made their way down her face. "Just like that?" she laughed indignantly. "Get over it? That's your answer to my problems?"

"Are you still that much in love with him that you would rather be miserable than to move on from the past? Were you always this type of woman— the one who lets the decisions of men control her emotions?"

Though his tone never changed, his words had cut worse than that of a dull blade, rugged and sharp they slit past all of her pretenses, all of her facades, all of the airs that she put on for the sake of her pride. For him to think that she was still in love with Todd was bad enough, but for him to question the validity of the pain she felt— having had to leave everything, and everyone she loved behind . . . the idea of being in love with Todd didn't even cross her mind. It wasn't Todd that she missed— it was her sisters, her family, and the idea that they hadn't loved her as much as she had loved them. It was the safety that a person should be able to feel in the presence of their loved ones that she no longer felt. In the home she had grown up in she felt like a stranger. That is what broke her heart, that is what caused her pain.

"You don't know me at all," she whispered.

Closing the distance between them Nicholas said, "Answer my question. Do you still love him?" He needed an answer. The idea that she still may have had feelings for the other man brought on an onset of emotions that he wasn't quite used to feeling. Jealousy had never been something he had to deal with, being that he always succeeded in acquiring his conquest, and happened to be the one who decided when relationships ended and other ones began. Yet for the first time he was truly getting a feel of what the crippling emotion felt like. His fingers tingled in anticipation of her response. Desperately needing to hear her reject his words Nicholas pushed the issue unwilling to let up. "Answer my question," he repeated, his voice barely an octave.

Charlotte inhaled deeply. The smell of his cologne filled her nostrils clouding her senses, enveloping her in all that was Nicholas. Closing her eyes she let out a slow breath working to gain control over her thoughts as his closeness worked at shattering her control.

"Dimple," he whispered, gently lifting her chin so that they were face to face. His silver eyes were warm as they gleamed at her. "Do you still love him?"

Charlotte moved then, wrapping her small fingers around his neck she pulled his head down to hers, pressing her lips against his with an urgency, a hunger unknown to her. A whispered moan slipped past her lips when he opened up to her allowing her tongue entrance into his mouth. With greedy fingers she tugged at his shirt, quickly pulling the material over his head before moving to his belt buckle. Heat engulfed her body spreading from one end to the next as her most sensitive peak swelled from a need she had never felt before. Unbuckling his pants with one hand Nicholas easily lifted Charlotte off the floor, pushing her against the wall with a roughness he hadn't intended. "Tighten your legs around my waist," he ordered as he stepped out of his jeans, his hands already pushing her dress up to rest at her hips. Charlotte did as she was told gasping when she felt his hand cup her heat. Nicholas stopped then. "Are you okay?" he asked breathing heavily, his forehead resting against hers.

"Yes," she whispered.

Tilting his head back he looked her in the eyes. "Liar," he breathed, placing her back onto the floor and reaching for his pants.

"What are you doing?" Charlotte asked, blinking at him, confusion paramount in her wide brown eyes.

She looked up at him with such innocence, Nicholas couldn't help but to bend his head and kiss her once more. "We can't do this," he murmured against her lips.

"Did I do something wrong?" she frowned, feeling slighted.

Grabbing his shirt off the floor he let out a sigh of frustration as he pulled the material over his head. "No," he answered, simultaneously patting his pants pockets for his car keys.

"Are you leaving?" she huffed, completely beside herself.

"We were seconds away from having sex. Literally seconds away. I had no intentions on stopping, and that makes me an asshole because your first time should be with someone you're in love with . . . it should be special. Not against a wall with my pants at my ankles and your panties pushed to the side . . . I just need to clear my head. I'll be back," he promised, kissing her forehead before leaving her alone in the quietness of her apartment to fixate over her thoughts. *My first time? How does he know that I've never . . . .* Resting her head against the wall she closed her eyes to the pain of rejection. His words radiating in her mind like crystalline on sand. 'Your first time should be with someone you're in love with.' "But I'm in love with you," she admitted aloud in the emptiness of the room, her gaze drifting to the topaz diamond that complimented her left hand. It fit so comfortable she all but forgot it was there. Exhaling deeply, Charlotte slid the gold band from her ring finger, her left palm instantly forming a vise- like grip around the band. It amazed her, how, in such a short amount of time the jewelry had left such a deep imprint, a *dimple*.

Like the newly born blossoms on the eve of spring morning, awaiting the Sun's unrequited first kiss, Charlotte allowed the realization to settle within her. She was in love with him.

Chapter Twenty One

Charlotte groaned at the loud humming noise sounding from her phone as the device vibrated against her nightstand. Glancing at the alarm clock she sighed aloud. *5:23 a.m. Seriously?* Flipping around in her large bed she pulled her comforter over her head. Fighting in vain to ignore the sound she squeezed her eyes shut in hopes of gaining a few more hours of sleep. Just then her house phone began to ring. "Leave me alone!" She squealed, covering her ears with her small hands until the answering machine picked up. *Seriously!*

"Charlotte, it's mom! Merry Christmas! Is Nick there with you? The oddest thing, I found his mother on that social media site you kids get on, rather Adeline found her. I sent her an email–"

"Inbox!" Adeline yelled in the background.

"Oh, that's right. That's right. I sent her an inbox," Babet laughed. "All of these different terms, geez, it's still a message no matter how you look at it. Anyway, you and that fiancé of yours has some explaining to do . . . his mother knew nothing of your engagement. She was shocked to even hear that her son was dating, let alone in the process of planning a wedding. We were chatting all night. She invited us to the Hamptons for the New Year, and I told her that it was a splendid idea. The Hamptons in the winter time− I can only imagine how beautiful it'll be. Give Nick a kiss for me, and we'll see you two in four days. Love you Charli!"

"Love you Charli," Adeline yelled, laughter in her voice.

Charlotte jumped out of bed quickly making her way to the living room where Nicholas had been sleeping soundly on her couch. "Wake up!" she screamed, poking him with quick fingers. "Wake up!"

"What?" he groaned, turning away from her.

"Wake up!" she gushed, frantically pulling the comforter off of him. "My mom contacted your mom on Facebook!"

Nicholas let out a long breath. "What?"

"You heard me. My mom told your mom that we're engaged, and your mom wants all of us to get together in the Hamptons for New Years," Charlotte said in a rush. "What are we going to do?"

"Don't worry so much. I'll tell my mother the truth, and she'll cancel with your folks," he answered, covering his face with his arm. "Give me the covers back."

"Nicholas, I can't let you do that. They are messaging each other now . . . your mom will tell my mother the truth, and then I'll look like a liar."

"You are a liar," he sighed, reaching for the covers.

"Not on purpose . . . I just wanted to save face after being humiliated. I didn't think that it would go this far," she moaned. "You can't tell your mom," she repeated.

Nicholas sat up rubbing his tired eyes with practiced patience. "So, what now? You want me to lie to my parents, too?"

"We got through Christmas . . . we can get through New Years and then before Valentine's Day we can just tell our families that we called off the wedding for uncontrollable differences."

"Dimple . . . after yesterday do you think we should keep–"

"Do you want me to beg because I will, please, just this one last time and I promise I will never ask you to lie for me again. Please."

Charlotte stood in front of him with her emotions on her sleeves, and panic in her eyes. How was he supposed to say no to that? "Okay."

"Really?" she gasped, falling to her knees in front of him.

"We're already in over our heads . . . why not?"

"Thank you," she breathed, elated.

"Merry Christmas, Dimple," he said, bending down to kiss her forehead.

"Merry Christmas."

ABOUT THE AUTHOR

Kristi Tailor, born and raised in Baltimore, Maryland earned her Bachelor's degree in English from Notre Dame of Maryland University. Her greatest joy in life is her young daughter Madison, who like her mother enjoys the art of storytelling. With a love for education and a passion for writing, Kristi spends her time combining the two with the hope of positively touching others with her life's work.